The Secret Adve1

Book ∠

'The Chilvester Passage'

By Debi Evans

Illustrations by Chantal Bourgonje

Published by Debi Evans
First Edition published in 2014
Printed by Biddles
Blackborough End, Norfolk

Copyright © Debi Evans 2014
Cover design & all illustrations Copyright © Chantal Bourgonje 2014

ISBN   9780992825720

For Gareth
Motivator and Dog Trainer.
Rolo does all his own stunts.
No animals were harmed during the writing of this
book.

For anyone new to the series, Rolo is a rescued Jack Russell and also 'the chosen one', discovering he has the ability to time travel via a hidden passage in an oak tree whenever he brings his pink ball, under the direction of Athelstan, guardian of the forest.

Rolo travels back through history in secret and always at night, to witness and sometimes influence events - Unbeknown to his owners: the smiley lady and the floppy haired boy, who wonder why their lovable pet is often tired during the day!

Life with Rolo is a constant adventure and I am assured he has many stories to tell so there are more books to come.

You can follow him on Twitter @rolodogblog and listen to his podcasts. He also has a Facebook page 'rolodogblog' and would appreciate a 'like'!

www.debievans.com

Contents

Prologue

Chapter 1   The Big Storm

Chapter 2   Blockage

Chapter 3   Rolo and the Tudor Ship

Chapter 4   Rolo and the Faithful Hound

Chapter 5   The Chilvester Passage

Chapter 6   Rolo finds Hope

Chapter 7   Rolo and the Moonrakers

Chapter 8   Hope Revisited

Chapter 9   Rolo and the World Cup Theft

Chapter 10   Forgiveness and Restoration

Chapter 11   Rolo on the Case

Chapter 12   Rolo and the Sphinx

Chapter 13   Rolo Recognised

Chapter 14   Rolo meets Shakespeare

Chapter 15   Rolo and the Black Death

Chapter 16   Rolo in Space

Chapter 17   Rolo and the X-Rays

Chapter 18   Rolo and the Amesbury Archer

Chapter 19   Rolo and the Art Thief

www.debievans.com

The Secret Adventures of Rolo

Book 2

The Chilvester Passage

Prologue

The massive slobbery mountain dogs were almost upon me…I was running in fear of my life!

I could feel their hot breath and almost taste their drooling saliva as they were gaining on me. I was deep within the forest and had nowhere to hide.

There were two of them and the pack instinct had kicked in. Pursuers and prey. There would be no reasoning with these monster dogs; this was not the time to turn round and give them a deferential lick under the chin.

If they caught me, I knew I would be torn to pieces.

Suddenly I realised where I had fled to, in my desperation to find sanctuary. We were close to the Athelstan tree. One minute I was in the forest playing with my pink ball which the floppy haired boy had thrown ahead for me to fetch, and the next minute I was being hunted down by these ferocious lion-type dogs that had appeared from nowhere. The floppy haired boy had vanished; forgotten in the fear and flight.

I threw myself under the bushes and felt a monster close its teeth around my back leg. When he opened his jaw to draw breath I managed to prise my leg out and fling

The Secret Adventures of Rolo

myself into the protection of the time tunnel. Thank goodness I still had the pink ball in my mouth; the gateway opened and gave me access. Safe at last.

I heard the floppy haired boy anxiously calling 'Ro-lo' as he ran to find me.

A tall and strong man appeared from nowhere and retrieved his lion dogs, firmly restraining them with choker chain leads around their pulsating necks; admonishing them as he secured them. The dogs had lost interest now their quarry had disappeared and they seemed calmed by his voice.

Athelstan was invisible. I kept very still within the tree, and when the man had taken his lion dogs away, both now acting like innocent lambs, I counted to ten and then scampered in the opposite direction as fast as I could to find the boy with floppy hair.

I glanced back up at Athelstan and he winked from the shadow of the bark. Our secret was still safe. All was as it should be. The time tunnel lay undiscovered.

Chapter 1

The Big Storm

I lay huddled in my basket, shaking all over, as we terriers sometimes do. There was a terrible commotion going on outside the kitchen window and I was genuinely scared. Everything out there was black as coal except for an occasional flash of light.

I'm sorry to say I just couldn't help myself- I started to howl.

The smiley lady came downstairs at once in her wrap-around dressing gown, rubbing her eyes as she opened the kitchen door murmuring soothing words to calm her petrified little dog. She didn't appear to be angry even though it was the middle of the night. Perhaps she couldn't sleep either. I hadn't made that kind of noise since I'd first come home and taken some time to settle in my new environment. Like any mother, the moment she heard me she instinctively knew

The Secret Adventures of Rolo

that something was wrong.

The smiley lady turned the key in the lock and opened the back door expecting me to scamper outside and run barking down the garden as I always do.

Being noisy as I run down the garden steps is my attempt at bravery as I usually bark when I am scared to warn the makers of noises in the dark that I am a big fierce dog and that they are on MY patch.

But tonight I wouldn't set as much as a paw out of the door. No amount of encouragement would entice me over the threshold. And no wonder.

There was a terrific storm raging in the sky all around us.

I glanced down the steps at the garden arch, so sweetly covered in honeysuckle and clematis a few months earlier in the summer. The arch was bending and twisting in the

fierce wind that threatened to carry it off beyond the back fence.

The young laburnum tree, only recently planted, was twisting and turning this way and that as though it were weeping and

The Secret Adventures of Rolo

wailing with its spindly branches sweeping the ground in lament.

The boundary fence creaked and groaned and the smiley lady was afraid it might fall over all together which would expose the rabbits huddled in their hutch in the next garden. I was too scared to even think about that exciting prospect just now. It was a fearsome night and no one could blame me for not wanting to venture outside.

A loud crack of thunder sent me cowering behind the smiley lady's legs and she counted out loud as she bent down to pick me up and cuddle me tight for comfort. On the count of four, a tremendous flash lit up the sky and she said, 'That means the storm is four miles away, Rolo.'

I felt strangely comforted by this knowledge although I couldn't convey this to the smiley lady, so I snuggled in closer to the warmth of her fleecy dressing gown, snuffling my nose into the thick pile.

Then the rain came. So powerful that it fell horizontally, lashing the back door and trying with all its might to come into the house. The smiley lady stepped backwards out of the doorway and closed it firmly, locking it once more.

'I don't blame you Rolo,' she said, realising I would not be heading out after all and scooping me up for another cuddle. Then she placed me carefully but firmly back in my basket and tucked my blanket around me and I heard the click of the kitchen door and her steady footfall as she took herself back upstairs to her own basket.

No sign of the owl; hopefully she was safely huddled in her nest and with any luck the woodland folk, Yulia and Da, were deep in the Understory and oblivious to the swirling chaos of the night.

The smiley lady slept in a bit longer in the morning than was usual after her disturbed night, and I was crossing my little furry legs by the time she came to open the kitchen door. I flipped over in my basket so she could give me my usual tummy rub greeting and then waited patiently for her to unlock the back door. Then I hurtled outside and came to a complete standstill at the top of the steps.

The sight that greeted us this chilly October morning was one of total devastation. The garden arch had indeed blown over; the broken clematis still clinging on for dear life, and the fence was leaning inwards at a very strange angle- I could almost see the rabbit hutch next door!

Leaves and twigs were strewn all over the steps. It was as if a whirlwind had struck late in one serious swoop, carrying away all the coverings of the trees that in Autumn usually took a much more gentle and prolonged attack to abandon their branches and drop to the floor.

The trees on the horizon looked to be

shivering; suddenly cold and bare.

The smiley lady put her hand to her mouth
in horror at the amount of tidying up that
would need to be done in the battered
garden. She would have to enlist the help
of the floppy haired boy who had of course
slept right through the storm. No sign of him
yet.

I sniffed around the garden, and drank from
a rain puddle. Everything smelt so fresh
and exciting! The vulnerable rabbits on the
other side of the falling fence would have to
wait. I wasn't sure if they were giggling or
whimpering.

To my surprise, the smiley lady soon called
me indoors, wiped my feet, and then she
gave me my doggy biscuit treat and picked
up her car keys. Terrified I was going to
be left behind, I ran to the front door and
huddled in the corner, blocking her exit and
doing my best meerkat impression, up on my
back legs, leaning on the door. How could

The Secret Adventures of Rolo

she resist me?

'Silly Rolo! Of course I'm taking you with me!' She picked up my lead from the hook by the door, wrapped a scarf around her neck and buttoned up her rain coat. This was a good sign. She locked the front door behind us, gathered her wellies from the porch and then bundled me into my travelling cage on the back seat of the car.

I could sense by the sounds of the engine and the changing scenery that we were driving up to my favourite place for a run- the other side of the forest, far away from the bottom of the garden.

Washed clean by the rain from the previous night, the forest would be an exciting place to explore in the daytime.

A final chug up the hill and we were there; I couldn't wait to be let out of the car and whimpered in excitement. The smiley lady was pulling on her wellingtons and didn't

The Secret Adventures of Rolo

bother to attach my lead. I ran to the nearest tree and stopped in surprise. My beloved forest resembled a war zone. Devastation everywhere, just like our back garden.

Young saplings were bent right over or snapped off. Big well-established trees had toppled like giants with their roots clinging stubbornly to the soil, making their bases as wide as their branch span.

It would be difficult for me to get to the Athelstan tree on the other side of the forest and I was worried about the guardian of the time tunnel. I wondered how he had fared in this terrible storm.

I could tell the smiley lady was just as shocked by this broken landscape.

We picked our way carefully over fallen branches and blocked paths. The sun shone weakly through the remaining upright branches but there were not many leaves to be seen. They were all sodden and dashed underfoot.

Like a ray of sunshine, a welcome sight on four legs came bounding towards me; I recognised the waggy tail and small brown and white face immediately. It was Chickpea, who the smiley lady calls 'my girlfriend' – well she's a friend and she's a girl so I suppose she is. We look pretty similar.

Our two owners exchanged pleasantries and discussed the carnage of the storm. Chickpea's owner was clad in Lycra as she is far more energetic than the smiley lady and runs everywhere rather than walks, so she had already seen more of the widespread storm damage.

The Secret Adventures of Rolo

Chickpea and I did a little square dance around each other in greeting and she whispered that she'd seen the other side and that all areas had been affected.

Upon hearing this news I was even more worried about the Athelstan tree. I made a plan to meet Chickpea later. The smiley lady wiped my muddy paws, bundled me back in the car and took me home for breakfast.

Dog Blog #1 — According to Rolo

I'm writing my dog blog whilst my people are clearing up after breakfast. I have to use their laptops whenever they are not looking. They don't know that I blog. In fact there's quite a lot about me that they don't know…the time travelling for instance.

A little bit more about Chickpea. She lives in a house with a cat.

At first sight the cat appears to be enormous, but it's actually all fur. It's very full of its own sense of self importance. Can you imagine more of a nightmare than living with a cat?

The only good thing about this arrangement, as far as I can see, is that there is a cat flap and Chickpea, being quite small, can use it to get in and out of the house whenever she likes.

Once I followed her into her house and had a fight with the cat. It almost ran up the curtains. I'd been out for a walk with the smiley lady and we found Chickpea wandering in the fields by herself. We took her home and her family were bemused that we'd returned her as she was quite used to wandering about on her own. Quite an independent little lady!

I have a few other canine chums living in the neighbourhood. We share the same walks and chase the same tennis balls.

There's Jasper, a brown Spaniel; we have our ups and downs. Then there's Merlin. He's a black Labrador/Springer cross and the smiley lady says he has the most expressive and intelligent face ever (me excepted of course). He is obsessed with playing ball and waits patiently even whilst his owners are in mid conversation, never once taking his eye off the ball, waiting for it to be thrown, and he ALWAYS brings it back and drops it to order.

23

When I first met Merlin two years ago he was a puppy and we were the same size. Somehow he's grown and grown and grown and...well, I haven't.

I always know when Merlin's about because the first thing I see is a black shadow passing overhead blotting out the daylight as he leaps over me.

If Merlin has a ball in his mouth he'll wave it in my face and urge me to chase him. He always gives it to me. He has such a sweet nature, but alas he is too big to fit in the time tunnel so he can never come adventuring with me. It's a shame as he would be quite useful and he is very obedient. Unlike Chickpea who is her own boss.

Then there's the General. He's a
pointer and very very tall. He
wants us all to defer to him and
most of the other dogs do, but I
try to get him to lick MY chin by
hanging off his back leg at every
opportunity. He usually manages to
shake me off with a disdainful look
on his face. The smiley lady is
always embarrassed when we meet the
General and his owners so she tries
to avoid confrontation by changing
our route whenever she can. We've
had a few run-ins, the General and
I.

As soon as the smiley lady had tucked me
into my basket that night, I opened the
cupboard under the kitchen sink and moved
the cleaning stuff and bucket to reveal the
secret trapdoor which took me outside. I
crept down the recently swept steps. She
must have put the floppy haired boy to work

The Secret Adventures of Rolo

earlier in the day whilst I was having a little doze on the back of the settee; I missed all that activity.

I squeezed under the gate and started trotting along the familiar path to the clearing behind the bushes, where the Athelstan tree proudly stood.

Scrabbling in the undergrowth to get to the clearing, I heard a sound and cocked an ear up. The next thing I knew I was flipped over onto my back and was rolling in the wet leaves with a small assailant on top of me. It was Chickpea!

'Hello Rolo! I wondered if I might catch you…what do you get up to in the forest at night? I've followed you here before and then you seem to…well, disappear. Do tell.'

I flipped Chickpea over so I was in charge and we roughed and tumbled a bit more and then both jumped up at the same time and stood nose to nose, four- square, staring each other out. It was a familiar game. She was a sneaky little thing – fancy Chickpea following me into the forest and me not even noticing!

I knew I could trust her, so I bade her follow me and we snuffled through the undergrowth…but to my dismay the clearing too had changed beyond recognition.

The Athelstan tree seemed to have taken the brunt of the storm. It was hemmed in on all sides by fallen trees; most of them young saplings.

I called to Athelstan and heard the familiar voice wheezing faintly through the broken branches.

'Rolo is that you? Come closer little pup, I can't quite see you…something is blocking my vision…who is that with you?' said the barky voice.

I clambered over some twigs and knocked

The Secret Adventures of Rolo

away a snapped branch that seemed to
be causing Athelstan some discomfort as
it was poking right in his eye, and then I
introduced Chickpea who was staring up
with awe at the kindly dragon face above
her. I had to nudge my companion as her
mouth was gaping open and I thought it was
impolite of Chickpea to stare.

'What on earth happened? Are you hurt?'
I asked with concern in my voice, once
Chickpea had clamped her jaw shut.

Athelstan lamented 'I told them it was
coming but they wouldn't listen…the wise
old oaks and beeches thought they could
withstand the storm and they dug their tree
roots in hard and girded themselves but
nothing could hold out against the might
of the wind last night….we lost a few old
ones …even Steady Stan over there…he's
stood beside me in the forest for hundreds of
years…never thought I'd see the day…'

We looked in the direction he was indicating

and saw a huge uprooted beech like a giant cotton reel lying in the forest floor.

'What about the young trees?' I asked, casting my eye around the scene of carnage. Saplings lay intertwined in a heap on the ground like an old fashioned game of Jack Straws. 'I thought they would have just bent a bit and sprung back!'

Athelstan took up the story in a sorrowful tone,

'The young trees were laughing at first, jostling about in the exhilaration of the storm; catching the wind in their young scrawny twigs…but the storm became more violent and they soon stopped laughing.

'I begged them to listen to me; to stand firm and dig in and embrace each other for strength but my warning was lost in the howling of the wind and they all went down like a pack of dominoes. There was nothing I could do but stand by and witness the

29

The Secret Adventures of Rolo

horror.'

Athelstan was clearly very upset by the loss of his domain.

There was more…

'Rolo have you brought the orb?' I knew he meant the pink ball, necessary for entering the time tunnel.

Chickpea looked around wondering what this strange dragon in the tree was talking about. In my fervour to come I had forgotten the pink ball and had left it in my basket. I said as much to the distraught guardian.

'Well never mind, it wouldn't do you any good anyway- the entrance to the time tunnel is blocked and I've heard that men with machines are coming tomorrow to saw logs and try to clear up some of this mess.'

Chickpea nudged me. Her brown eyes were as round as tea plates. I could see I had some explaining to do. It sounded as if I wouldn't be able to time travel for a while. It seemed as if Athelstan read my thoughts.

'There is another way little pup…but you have to find it….' His barky voice faltered. I wondered where on earth I was to start looking. Then I suddenly thought of the woodland folk.

'What of Yulia and Da? Are they alright?' I voiced my concerns.

'I haven't seen them. I would think they are safe within the Understory,' the wise tree dragon said, shaking his head sadly.

'Come on Rolo, we'd better be getting home before we are missed,' said Chickpea, nudging me, and I could sense I was in for a grilling from this inquisitive female Jack Russell on the way home.

'Pleased to have met you,' said a mere shadow of Athelstan as he faded into the bark and there was nothing else for it but to head homeward with a heavy heart.

I wondered how much I should tell Chickpea, but I needn't have worried. My doggy sense told me that she was completely trustworthy.

Chickpea is slightly smaller than me, a bit wild and, dare I say, a little older. I know it's indelicate to talk about a lady's age so we'll pass over that. She's pretty fit though in the old fashioned sense of the word as she is always out running with her owners; unless she sees me, of course, then she hangs back and we pass the time together, and they pick her up on the way home from their circular run. Anyway she can get in and out of the house by means of a cat flap. That's pretty neat- well except for living with a cat of course.

And so I found myself telling Chickpea on the way home about my secret life and she didn't believe me at first. I told her about my adventures with the cat in the Marlborough fire, the English Civil War, the boy in the Blitz, the invention of Cats Eyes, Vesuvius erupting and the Montgolfier balloon ride, and she looked at me in awe.

Of course she wants to come with me next time I time travel but I explained about the Athelstan tree being the only entrance to the time tunnel and we had both seen that there wouldn't be any adventures for a while; at least not until the forestry people had cleared some of the fallen trees.

We fell silent and I bade her goodnight as she peeled off to head to her own front door. The clatter of the cat flap meant she was safely inside. I went to bed with a heavy heart and wondered when I would next be able to go on an adventure. Athelstan's words were going round and round in my head: 'there is another way'. But what was it?

Chapter 2

Blockage

The next day passed in a flurry of activity. A nice long walk by the canal in Devizes with the smiley lady. Way too cold to jump in the water at this time of the year and the ducks knew it. They tormented me from the far side of the canal. I'm sure they were laughing at me. We walked back through the market square and the smiley lady stopped to read the inscription on the market cross.

This was the story of Louise Procter who, during Puritan times, tried to cheat about the weight of the sack of corn she was selling. 'May God strike me down if I am lying' she said and the next minute she was dead right there on the steps. The smiley lady found this fascinating and warned me never to cheat and lie. I sat patiently on the pavement, firmly attached to my lead gazing up at her and saying nothing. Sometimes I think it's a pity that I can't talk to humans in my everyday life, only when I time travel.

The next day the smiley lady and I went to the forest again through the back garden, and, hoping she wouldn't notice, I ran on ahead to see Athelstan. Before I'd reached the clearing I could hear the loud buzzing of chainsaws and there were several men in high visibility jackets, with helmets and heavy boots busily clearing the storm devastation.

I couldn't get close enough to Athelstan to see him but I could imagine he would be shrinking into the bark, afraid of injury and discovery.

The smiley lady spoke to one of the men and asked what he was doing. He appeared to be drawing symbols on some of the trees.

The Secret Adventures of Rolo

'Stand back, love, these are unsafe. The marked trees are the ones that have to come down,' the burly bearded man replied and she called me away at once from the danger area.

I glanced back over my shoulder as she clipped my lead on and saw the sight I was dreading; the man was drawing a cross on the Athelstan tree in bright orange chalk.

That could only mean one thing! The guardian of the time tunnel was condemned!

I heard the men confirming that the felling of the trees would begin the next day by contractors with the right equipment and that the area would be properly cordoned off to stop the public being injured during the dangerous but necessary process to make the forest safe.

We walked home and the smiley lady noticed there wasn't the usual spring in my step. Even my tail was drooping.

Night time couldn't come quickly enough for me; I didn't have any enthusiasm for the game of 'Hide The Biscuit', much to the floppy haired boy's disappointment, and I got into my basket long before I was told it was bedtime. At last the sounds of the house went quiet.

There was a tapping at the kitchen window. I had a night time visitor. The owl had come for me. Thank goodness she was all right. I assumed she lived in a tree that had not blown over.

She waited whilst I tried to open the secret trapdoor under the kitchen sink. It was stuck fast though and wouldn't budge. Something seemed to be blocking it from the other side! The owl fluttered impatiently at the window and then I could see Yulia clinging to her neck feathers. I climbed up onto the kitchen counter with the aid of a stool and edged my way carefully round the sink, moving geraniums on the windowsill so I could

37

converse with the tiny rider.

'Yulia! Something's blocking the trapdoor! Can you see what the problem is?' I shouted through the window in a stage whisper.

'There's a great big earthenware trough with the remains of the summer's strawberry plants in it!' mouthed Yulia in despair.

'It's way too heavy for me to shift!' she tailed off.

'Go and fetch Chickpea; she'll know what to do!' and I gave her instructions as to which house my little friend lived in.

Ten minutes later little Chickpea was puffing and panting and straining, putting her

The Secret Adventures of Rolo

stocky terrier shoulders into the task but she couldn't move the strawberry trough. I felt helpless, watching through the window. There was no way of rounding up the other dogs; they would be asleep in their baskets oblivious to the dilemma.

'It's no good…I can't get out.' I hung my head sadly.

'But you must!' said Yulia. 'The men are coming to chop down the Athelstan tree tomorrow…we're relying on you! We have to do something!'

I remembered the conversation the smiley lady had with the bearded man in the forest.

'You have to get rid of the marking on the Athelstan tree. The contractors who are bringing their power tools are only going to take out the trees that have the forestry chalk mark on them!'

Chickpea said at once 'I can do that' and I

had to stand helplessly in the kitchen sink with my paws on the window sill, watching as my best friend scampered down my garden steps, guided by Yulia and the owl, for the most important secret mission of her life. I fervently hoped she would be up to the task.

The next day, Jasper, Merlin and Chickpea and their owners came round for coffee and a chat with the smiley lady and we dogs were let out into the garden so we could run around.

When the coast was clear we created a diversion. The two bigger dogs chased a tennis ball behind the strawberry trough and Chickpea and I caused a bit of a scene as we mock fought pretending to retrieve it. This had the desired effect.

The smiley lady was watching through the kitchen window where she was amazed to discover a paw print on the sill. She rubbed at it with the dishcloth. Then, frowning, she

put down her coffee cup and with the help
of Jasper's owner they slid the strawberry
trough along about a foot, so we could get
the tennis ball out and continue our game.
The ladies barely paused for breath as they
continued their conversation, chattering
away like magpies.

I hardly dared look at Chickpea as she picked
up the ball in her mouth. The ladies went
back indoors without replacing the trough.
Unbeknown to the smiley lady, our plan had
worked and my trapdoor exit was clear once
more!

That night I raced to the Athelstan tree
without waiting to be summoned. I
remembered to take the pink ball. I wasn't
surprised that Chickpea, heroine of the hour,
was just behind me. I was relieved to see
the shadowy outline of the guardian in his
familiar pose, wrapped around the oak tree.
At least it was still upright.

'You're still here! I was so worried,' I blurted

out and the tree dragon smiled his

woody smile and said,

'All thanks to your little chum here; I wondered what on earth she was doing when she showed up with Yulia standing on her back and started rubbing wet leaves on my bark!'

'Well it was Rolo's idea,' blushed Chickpea, pleased to have proved useful.

'Your plan worked, Little Pup. Alas if you look around you, the condemned trees have indeed fallen, but I stand tall and proud: guardian of the forest once more. Little acorns will grow and new trees will spring up. All is not lost. I am in your debt.'

I ran to the base of the tree, eager to show Chickpea the entrance to the time tunnel she had helped to save, and then my face fell in dismay.

'It's blocked up with sawdust and bits of

wood; it will take ages to dig it out!'

I started scrabbling in the sawdust and then
Da stepped out from the shadows of the
tree roots, brushing his clothes down as he
harrumphed.

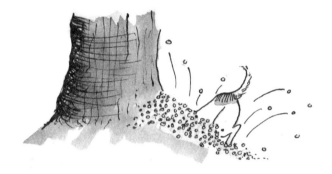

'Sorry Da! Didn't see you there!' I apologised
to the tiny woodland man whom I'd just
covered in sawdust.

'It's as well I'm good at digging!' I said,
getting straight back to the task once he was
clear.

'Don't you mean 'WE', said Chickpea, joining
in. Soon sawdust, leaves and twigs were
flying everywhere and Da and Yulia ducked

for cover.

Athelstan was actually laughing – the first time since the Big Storm that a smile had cracked his face. We Jack Russells flew to the task, digging with all our might, showing off in competition with each other.

44

We were eventually worn out, and sorry to see the digging had not made much impact on the blocked entrance other than to cover everything else in sawdust. Even Athelstan was sporting a wood chip beard!

'It's no use,' Da said, shaking his head. 'The sawdust has got right into the time tunnel and completely blocked the entrance. We'll have to find a new home. Not good for my asthma,' he wheezed.

Athelstan shook his dragony face until the wood chip beard fell to join the leaves on the forest floor. 'There is another way,' he repeated mysteriously, 'but you will have to find it. I can't help you.'

Da piped up, 'By the way, Paddy Paws, you need a lesson on tree identification because I don't think you know the difference between oaks, ashes and horse chestnuts, let alone sweet chestnuts, beech, silver birch and sycamores'.

Still wheezing, he laid a collection of leaves
on the ground. They looked like this:

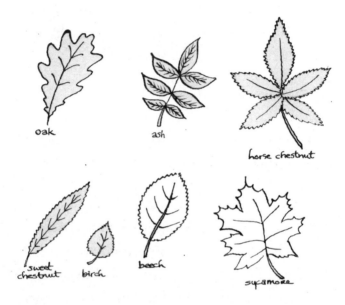

This goes to show that even when a storm
disrupts life in the forest, Da's nature lessons
still go on!

Just then the owl reappeared, swooping low
and she said something to Yulia which she
then passed on to Da. Both woodland folk
climbed on the owl's back, Yulia helping her
great great grandfather to take a firm hold of

The Secret Adventures of Rolo

the feathery taxi on the back of her neck.

'The owl will take us to her tree; she says we'll be safe in there,' Yulia shouted as the owl took off again having barely paused for breath. She didn't like to leave her babies unattended for too long.

Dog Blog #2— According to Rolo

The next day the smiley lady took me down to the High Street because she wanted to buy a birthday card. It was cold and blowy and she wrapped up well. I like market day as I am invariably given a doggy treat by one of the stall holders. I also like hoovering up the crumbs outside the bakers, where the builders and school children eat their pasties. I was not disappointed. The smiley lady tied me up outside a charity shop whilst she went card shopping, telling me

to be a good boy. I found myself
next to a large dog. It was a sort
of yellow Labrador. I tried to
have a conversation with it and
then realised it was fake. Further
investigation showed it was set on
a plinth with a slit in the top
where you are supposed to put coins
for animal charities. Silly me!
Sometimes I can be a dog of little
brain!

Chapter 3

Rolo and the Tudor Ship

In the afternoon the smiley lady and I set off on a different route, down to the chalk white horse and then up the hill on the other side of the valley known locally as Treacle Bolley.

I spied a large hole and the smiley lady walked on briskly, calling me to come but not really taking too much notice. Then she met another dog walker with a

Dalmation and was soon deeply engrossed in conversation and admiring the big black and white dog. The spotty dog eyed me suspiciously as I cautiously edged towards a foxhole nestling under the tree roots. It looked interesting.

He said, 'I wouldn't if I were you: you'll get stuck if you go in there, little dog.'

I told him politely to mind his own business and he went off in a sulk sniffing at cow pats. There was something very familiar about the tunnel- and not just the earthy smell.

My instincts told me this linked to the time tunnel. I saw a tiny flash of light and further investigation showed Yulia and Da hurrying by with their lanterns.

'Clever Paddy Paws!' said Yulia. 'Athelstan knew you'd find the other entrance! You'll need the pink ball though.'

'ROLO! RO-LO!' I could hear the smiley

lady calling me and when I backed out from the hole the spotty dog looked rather smug as if it had told on me. Little did he know that my adventures were about to begin again! I trotted back to the smiley lady and succumbed to her fondling my ears.

Napping in my basket during the afternoon the smiley lady noticed I was doing 'clown eyes'- that's when my eyes close into vertical lines and it always makes her and the floppy haired boy laugh. I was actually seeing canon fire in my dream!

I could hardly wait for the owl to summon me that night. I picked up the pink ball from its safe place under my basket.

'I've found another entrance!' I told her, and the brown winged bird flew overhead as I scampered down the hill and, when it was safe, I crossed the road and ran up the gulley on the other side, retracing my steps to the foxhole. Yulia was already waiting for me, lantern at the ready.

'You're off to sea. I hope you've got sea legs!"
said Yulia, and then she passed on Athelstan's
message.

The message made no sense to me.
Furthermore, I had to tell someone to leave a
sinking ship. I wondered if Yulia had got the
message right; it could be a bit like Chinese
Whispers lost in the re-telling.

Yulia and I spent most of the journey in the
narrow dark tunnels, talking about nature to
pass the time. I asked Yulia what she knew
of the owl family as I could never get much
conversation from the great brown bird.
Yulia told me that she had learned quite a
lot whilst they were lodging in the same tree
with the owl family. The owl's name was
Bubo.

Yulia said, 'Did you know that owls eat small
mammals whole, and larger prey needs to
be torn up to be eaten? That's why owls have
very sharp and powerful talons on the end of
their muscular legs.'

I must admit I don't know much about owls at all except that they come out at night, or are 'nocturnal' as Yulia corrected me.

Yulia went on, 'Unlike some other birds, when they eat owl food passes directly into the digestive system. Anything which isn't digestible at all, such as fur, bones, claws and feathers, gets filtered out via the gizzard and lays in a separate part of the stomach. Several hours after eating a meal, all these indigestible parts will be compressed into a pellet which will then be stored and up to ten hours later will be regurgitated and exits the owl's body through the beak.'

'So an owl pellet is really owl sick?' I said in fascination.

'No. It's not really spitting or vomiting. When the pellet is ready, the owl goes to its favourite roost on a tree or stump and closes its eyes with a rather pained expression on its face. The first time I saw Bubo do it I thought she was unwell and I watched with concern

53

as she stretched her neck up and forwards and suddenly a little circular disc popped out! Straight away afterwards she was back to normal,' Yulia explained.

The floppy haired boy would find all this really cool. Shame I can't share my knowledge with him!

'The other amazing thing about owls is their field of vision. Most birds have eyes on the side of their head but the reason the owl looks so 'wise' is because it has binocular vision which means it sees objects with both eyes at the same time. It also has three eyelids: the upper one for blinking, the lower one closes for sleeping and the middle one moves diagonally and acts like a windscreen wiper to keep the eye clean and protected.

'They can only look straight ahead, not roll their eyes at all, but to make up for that narrow field of vision they can turn their heads around some 270 degrees. They also have very acute hearing and fly with their

The Secret Adventures of Rolo

powerful wings swiftly in silent swoop very close to the ground, so their prey does not really stand a chance once an owl has it in their sights.'

Yulia had clearly learned a lot during her stay with the owl family.

We reached the end of the tunnel and Yulia waved me off, anxious to return to Da who was helping field mice sort out a housing shortage. I turned to watch her with her little lantern bobbing in the dark and the light becoming smaller and smaller as she retraced our steps in the tunnel. Then I realised I was in a sort of chamber and had to scamper up the wall of it on to a ledge to exit the tunnel.

The ground shook. It occurred to me that I had come out in a place that was moving. In fact it was lurching about violently from side to side. I had no idea where I was but I could definitely smell the salty smell of the sea. My nose twitched. I learned my lesson not to drink seawater last year in Devon! I had unpleasant memories of being very sick last time I drank a lot of it. I wouldn't make that mistake again!

Looking around at the timber frame I worked out that I was in the very bottom of a large wooden ship and, judging by the movement, I would say the sea was rough and, by the sound of it, we were in the midst of a battle. Every now and then there was a tremendous boom and the ship would roll and list a little, then right itself and then I would hear the boom again and lurch across the hold.

I didn't really have sea legs.

I was suddenly aware that I was not alone. There were two canine companions, skulking in the hold. Both dogs eyed me suspiciously and growled. They looked a little bit like me, I thought, perhaps a little taller.

One introduced himself as Hatch and the

other was called Cross. They seemed to me to be somehow quite old fashioned in the way they spoke to each other. I couldn't quite put my finger on it. A rat scurried past and Hatch sprang off in pursuit. I got the impression that Cross really couldn't be bothered.

'We are the King's rat catchers!' said Hatch rather triumphantly as he returned with a rat between his teeth.

Cross yawned. I asked which King that might be, as casually as I could, trying to ascertain exactly whereabouts in history I was on this adventure.

'Why, good sir, King Henry VIII of course!' said Hatch, scampering to the nearest porthole and with a neat flick of his head he dispatched the rat to its watery grave.

'What are you doing here anyway?' asked Cross, 'Are you my replacement?' he added rather hopefully. 'I've put in for a transfer.'

'I come with a message that when the time comes you are to abandon ship,' I said with as much authority as I could muster.

Hatch the rat despatcher snorted with laughter. 'Abandon ship? That's never going to happen!'

Cross said, 'It seems a very good idea to me, whoever you are and wherever the message has come from, I'm right behind you.'

What very strange and opposite dogs they were!

More canon fire, but to my cocked ear it all seemed to be coming from one side of the ship. Suddenly a gust of wind whipped up from nowhere and caught the sails and we wheeled round ninety degrees.

I was buffeted across the hold and careered into a canon which had fired and then shot back for reloading. I picked myself up, shook to check for damage.

I was fine and out from the corner of my eye I saw the outline of a rose on the canon. The words 'honi soit qui mal y pense' were written around it and there were two lion heads on the canon shaft itself.

'What ship is this?' I asked out of curiosity (Which, as we know, killed some animals).

My question went unanswered. The struck ship was turning but listing too. This time she could not right herself.

Hatch shouted, 'They've left the gunports open; the water is flooding into the canon doors; I suspect they added too many canons last time the ship went in for a refit. We're sinking!'

'We're doomed!' wailed Cross.

'Not if you both follow me,' I shouted over the tremendous roar of the sea, now pouring into the hold and lapping round my feet.

Fighting the increasing tide of flood water, I doggy paddled around the hold trying to find the entrance to the time tunnel. This was turning into a bit of a nightmare adventure. Several times I went under and thought I was destined to die at sea. The terrier called Cross was keeping very close to my tail and kept grabbing hold of it which hindered my swimming and nearly took me under.

At last I found the entrance and jumped in. It was a bit like a drain, and I landed in a shallow puddle of water. I then had to scramble up a sharp bank to enter the tunnel proper. Yulia backed away, shielding her lantern as I shook my wet coat.

'I've got someone with me – there were two dogs but only one would leave, the other wanted to stay with the sinking ship in the line of duty,' I spluttered.

'I think you'll find your companion won't be able to come to our century with you Paddy Paws; he will have to take his chances and swim,' Yulia said in a matter of fact voice as she turned to walk down the time tunnel back towards the 21st century foxhole.

'Wait, I have to see if he's alright,' I shouted, and without hesitation I plunged back into the u-bend at the end of the tunnel. The ship was floundering. I was in the open sea with guns firing around me! I rose to the surface to fill my lungs with air so I could descend

61

The Secret Adventures of Rolo

to the tunnel once more, and that's when I caught sight of Cross, doggy paddling away from the sinking ship, in the direction of land.

I managed to locate the end of the time tunnel for a second time, although it was just breaking away from the ship. Yulia was rather annoyed with me when I emerged through the u-bend and shook off the sea water giving her a soaking for the second time that evening.

Eventually reaching home, I crawled into my basket leaving a wet puddle on the floor. No doubt my people would think it was something other than seawater but I couldn't worry about that now. I was so exhausted and cold. A thoroughly damp dog. I used my teeth to pull my blanket over me and lay shivering for a while. I must have eventually dozed off.

The smiley lady opened the door and sniffed the air, opening the kitchen window to ventilate. Luckily the puddle had evaporated.

'Pooh!' she said wrinkling her nose. 'I think someone needs a bath.'

The floppy haired boy went on a school trip to Portsmouth Historic Dockyard during the following week and I was sorry to have been left behind. He came home with tales about the wonderful new Mary Rose exhibition. He told his mum about all the amazing treasures that had lain on the bottom of the sea in the hull of the shipwreck for almost five hundred years since its sinking in 1545.

'You wouldn't believe what they recovered from the Mary Rose, Mum; not only cannon balls but pewter tankards, plates, tables and chairs, coils of rope, chests, cannon, armour, clothes, shoes, food and drink barrels as well as a tremendous amount of hand held weapons from muskets to pikes, and an incredible amount of personal effects including money and jewellery!'

63

The Secret Adventures of Rolo

'I wonder how all this treasure survived in the sea for so long?' asked the smiley lady and the floppy haired boy knew all the answers from the exhibition,

'It was because of the way the ship lay on the sea bed, half submerged in the silt. That's why half the timbers are so well preserved too, because they were buried in the sand and not damaged by the shifting water.'

'How did they identify the wreck as being Henry Vlll's flag ship when they found it then?'

'Well, divers found a canon with the Tudor rose on it and the motto of the 'Order of the Garter' which is 'honi soit qui mal y pense' proving it was a royal ship and they knew roughly where to look from historic records of the sinking.'

He added, 'Did you know, Mum, that when they floated the wreck of the Mary Rose up the Solent on a cradle supported by giant air bag raft in 1982, they spent the next thirty years gently spraying the timber with sea water otherwise sudden exposure to the air might have made the wood fall apart immediately.'

'The wonders of modern technology' murmured the smiley lady, pleased that her son had actually listened and learned something from this school trip.

'I remember watching the raising of the Mary Rose on the television; it truly was a tremendous sight. I'll never forget it,' she added.

From underneath the dining room table, no one saw the double take I did when the floppy haired boy reached into his backpack and brought out a sketch of 'Hatch' purchased in the gift shop. It was an artist's interpretation of what the skeleton of the dog found in the wreck near one of the cabins might have actually looked like. Not a bad likeness, I thought.

The Secret Adventures of Rolo

'Don't you think he looks a bit like Rolo?' the floppy haired boy held the picture up for his mum to see.

'Why on earth would they have had a terrier on board a ship?' asked the smiley lady.

'To keep the rat population down, I guess.' He turned to me and stroked my ears roughly, 'What do you think Rolo? Would you like to be a rat catcher at sea?'

Not on your nelly, I thought to myself. No mention in the Dockyard exhibition of Hatch's fellow rat catcher then; it seemed that I was the only one that knew that there had been two terriers on board the Mary Rose, as only one dog's remains were found. I could only assume that Hatch made it to terra firma and hoped that the lazy dog had lived to tell the tale. I couldn't help wondering if I'd saved the right dog…

The Secret Adventures of Rolo

Chapter 4

Rolo and the Faithful Hound

A few weeks later, Athelstan summoned me via Bubo owl. I looked at her with a new respect, willing her to spin her head round or cough up a pellet but of course she never did when she was working. I'd had a vision of a baby during an afternoon nap.

Yulia told me that this was to be a very important mission, way back to the 13th century to a place called Gwynedd in North Wales. I asked if Chickpea might be able to come along as she was dying to go on a time travelling adventure ever since she'd found out about the Athelstan tree. Yulia didn't think it would be a problem but flew back to check with Athelstan whilst I alerted Chickpea.

I didn't have to go and knock for her; she was already hanging around outside the garden gate. By that time the owl and tiny rider reappeared with confirmation that it was all right for her to accompany me this time, as Chickpea had been instrumental in saving the Athelstan tree.

We had already found another pink ball so that she would be able to enter the time tunnel, and were soon on our way to the foxhole entrance on Treacle Bolley.

I'd worked out during my daily walks that the foxhole was not that far underground from the main entrance of the time tunnel through the Athelstan tree. That entrance was still blocked and so I could only get my instructions from Athelstan or via Yulia, and then use the foxhole entrance to access the time tunnel.

Chickpea was as excited as I had been on my first time travelling adventure, and the two of us powered through the tunnel, adrenalin rushing, wondering what was in store for us at the other end.

'Steady on you two!' remonstrated Yulia as we raced neck and neck.

At the end of the tunnel, however, I slowed right down and prepared to exit with some trepidation. I had come to learn that travelling back to different times could be quite dangerous; you never knew what you were going to meet at the other end. Chickpea in her innocence was not scared at all and eager to taste adventure. She kept urging me on.

I shouldered her out of the way.

Barely setting paw outside the tunnel, I was set upon by a monstrous beast. All went dark and I could only assume the assailant had my head clamped firmly in its mouth! I could taste hot slobbery breath and had a flashback to the lion dogs that had chased me into the Athelstan tree, and I thought I was done for as my life flashed in front of my eyes.

Luckily Chickpea was there – she was small

but mighty and totally unafraid of whatever it was that was trying to kill her companion!

Without giving thought to her own safety, she jumped on the beasts back and sunk her teeth into its hind quarters and, as the angry black shadow swung around to attack his assailant, I found the pressure of its jaws easing and I managed to wriggle out of its grasp.

Chickpea was still hanging off its back end, but she was quick witted enough to know when to remove her powerful little jaws, once she knew I was free. The two of us shot back into the tunnel entrance, leaving the assailant howling and licking his wounds as it limped away.

We heard a twig snapping nearby and were scared for a moment that it might be another beast, but instead we spied a tall hound with a kindly and intelligent face. His gentle features reminded me a bit of our friend Merlin. We cautiously stepped out of the tunnel entrance for the second time; Chickpea was right behind me.

'Bore Da,' the hound spoke softly in Welsh. I recognised this greeting from my puppyhood and was able to respond. The hound introduced himself as Gelert and he was very concerned for our wellbeing. He could see my neck was bleeding a little. We explained about the beast and he thanked us for the warning.

The kindly hound then led us to a small clearing, where he showed us that he was watching over a human baby whilst his royal master was out hunting. Chickpea put her paws up on the crib and leaned in, admiring the sleeping infant. Neither of us had seen such a tiny human baby before.

Suddenly the black beast reappeared, springing from behind a tree and determined to avenge his wounds and his pride. He tipped the cradle up and the baby fell to the floor.

Without hesitation, I threw my body underneath and managed to soften the infant's fall and amazingly he didn't even wake up as I lay him gently on the ground.

Whilst Gelert and Chickpea attacked the predator, I carefully manoeuvred the upended crib over the sleeping babe to shelter him. My intention was to keep the human baby secret and safe.

Then I joined the melee. It didn't take the three of us very long to finish off the silent dark assassin. Gelert dealt the final death blow, biting the beast's neck, and the huge body slumped to the ground and lay there like a rug.

Just at that moment, a trumpet blast heralded the return of Prince Llewellyn and his hunting party. Gelert was so pleased to hear his master's voice that he ran up to him, putting his big paws up on the prince's chest and pushed his head forward, waiting for the familiar ear rub greeting.

Prince Llewellyn's eyes surveyed the scene and all he could see was the upturned cradle and his beloved dog whose jaws were dripping with blood and he immediately jumped to the wrong conclusion.

It was as if we were in a play. Time seemed frozen. None of us could move. The Prince was the first to react.

He unsheathed his sword and was about to kill his beloved dog by plunging his sword right through his ribcage when the baby's muffled cries could be heard from beneath the crib.

The spell was broken and Chickpea couldn't stand back any longer; she ran forward and flipped the covering over to reveal the mewling baby. I jumped up at the Prince and tugged at his sleeve, shouting that all was well; Gelert had slain the beast and saved the baby.

Thank goodness the Prince lowered his

sword arm and released his hold on the
startled hound.

Prince Llewellyn listened to my explanation
and finally his eyes rested on the carcass of
the slain beast.

'A wolf!' he cried. 'You brave dogs have saved
my baby from this savage wolf!'

Phew, that was close...if we hadn't been
there at that moment, I felt sure the Prince
would have done away with his dog! Instead
he called him 'Faithful Hound' and publicly
honoured his courage in saving the tiny heir
to the throne. Chickpea and I sneaked off
back to the time tunnel, leaving Gelert to
enjoy the praise.

75

The Secret Adventures of Rolo

'Nos da,' I whispered, but it went unanswered. I liked testing out languages. Once more I thought how lucky it was that I could communicate with humans in my time travelling adventures. It was such a pity I couldn't do this in my daily life!

'Quite enough excitement for one night I think!' I said to Chickpea, whose eyes were positively sparkling from the exhilaration of this adventure. We bade goodnight to Yulia at the foxhole and went our separate ways, each to our own basket before the sun rose and a new day dawned.

Chapter 5

Rolo and the Chilvester Passage

The next morning the smiley lady was concerned about the slight gash I had around my neck, and she put a towel on the draining board and lifted me up for a closer look. She then washed it gently with mild antiseptic. The smiley lady wondered out loud where I might have got it from ('it looks like a bite') and she said I looked a bit tired. Then we set out for a walk on my lead, down the hill and along the High Street, and for once, the boy with floppy hair was with us.

Both humans had check-up appointments with the dentist and so they took it in turns to go into the surgery, and whoever wasn't in the chair having their mouth examined, had to stand outside with me as dentists don't seem too keen on having dogs in their surgery. I peered through the window.

I would have liked to have had a ride in the

cool chair and had my teeth counted by a lady wearing rubber gloves and a mask. If you remember, I lost one corner tooth whilst giving a tug to the secret trapdoor under the sink when I first discovered it last year.

It seems the dentist is not very dog friendly. She's probably a cat person. Bah!

On our way back home we stopped in the redundant church (where I **am** allowed to go inside) and the smiley lady and floppy haired boy chose a piece of homemade cake each (coffee and walnut for the smiley lady and carrot cake for the floppy haired boy).

'Very healthy after the dentist,' I thought, but kept it to myself as I was given a water bowl and a doggy biscuit for being a good boy.

St Peters is a very old church, dating back beyond Tudor times – you may recall I had an adventure during the ordination of Thomas Wolsey. For now, my lead was firmly tied to a chair leg. I settled down.

Glancing at some exposed bricks on the crumbling plaster-covered wall behind the grand piano, I found myself thinking the wall had stood there for a very long time indeed and must have seen some comings and goings.

It was then that I noticed a patch of missing plaster, and the floppy haired boy followed my gaze and I'm sure we saw the same thing at exactly the same time.

The Secret Adventures of Rolo

On the wall, clear as anything, was
the outline of a dog's profile in the old
brickwork, and I have to say it looked pretty
much like a portrait of yours truly. Of course
I couldn't say any of this out loud, but I
sat staring at it with my feet gathered in,
whilst the floppy haired boy drew his mum's
attention to it.

'Oh I say…it looks just like Rolo!' she
exclaimed, last to notice.

The floppy haired boy untied my lead from
the chair leg and led me over to see my
likeness on the wall.

I can't really describe what happened next
except to say I had a strange feeling creep
all over my fur…I suppose it was what you
might call 'goose bumps'. This dog mural
needed further investigation, but not now,
and not with my people.

I spied a fire exit near the altar and it looked
like the wood at the bottom of the door had

rotted away. Someone had placed a plank of wood over it to keep the draughts out. I would have to come back later for a closer look at the mural, and that door could be my way in, under the cover of darkness.

We had a fairly uneventful afternoon. I barked at the postman and sniffed around at the falling fence with the rabbits huddled in their hutch behind it. The smiley lady said she really must alert the neighbours as to the state of their fence.

I couldn't sleep for thinking about the dog on the wall.

Later that night, when the sounds of the house had gone quiet, I kicked off my blanket and crept out through my secret trapdoor and ran down the hill as fast as I could to the old church. The High Street was silent, shops shuttered, businesses closed up for the night, and residents tucked up in bed with curtains firmly drawn. The silver moonlight shone on the church clock on the bell tower and showed the time to be just a little before midnight.

I skirted round the outside of the church keeping close to the walls and found my way to the end of the church with the biggest stained glass window and I soon found the door with the rotten wood at the bottom.

I nudged at the plank of wood with my nose and it fell with a clatter. I squeezed under the small dog-sized gap. I was inside, at the right end of the church. All was quiet, save the chiming of twelve.

The helpful moonlight threw beams of light onto the flagstone floor, and where the light came through the stained glass windows it made pools of rich colour on the Minton tiles. No time to investigate that now; I was drawn to the dog mural on the wall next to the chancel, behind the piano. I crossed the transept and approached it on tiptoe as my claws made a skittering noise on the tiles interrupting the silence of the church.

As the last stroke of midnight rang out, an eerie glow surrounded the dog on the wall like a halo and I moved in closer. It yawned open in the blackness; a dog shaped passage way and just my size.

The passage smelt musty and damp, twice as pungent as the odour of old church buildings. I was hesitant about taking the next step and actually crossing the threshold.

I pushed my nose in and wrinkled it. To my surprise, a tiny glow flickered just inside the passage way. It was Yulia! Boy was I pleased to see her! I called out to her and she waved her lantern.

The Secret Adventures of Rolo

'Paddy Paws, you found it; Athelstan said you would! We weren't allowed to help! Clever boy finding it all by yourself.'

'Where are we Yulia? What is this passage? Is it another entrance to the time tunnel?' I was so excited that all my sentences ran into each other.

'Slow down Paddy Paws, one thing at a time. Come inside, and don't be scared. I will light your way, just as before.

'This is the Chilvester Passage. Athelstan knew you would find it, and he has a very urgent important job for you. Come quickly and I'll show you.'

'Where am I going Yulia? Does it link to the time tunnel? What's the mission?' I asked eagerly, trying to take in the new surroundings and keeping an ear up in the gloom of the tunnel in case of sound, following Yulia's pin prick of light swinging as she strode on ahead.

'You will know when you get there,' she replied mysteriously and I felt as if I could be talking to Athelstan himself.

I followed the tiny light through the dark passage and wondered where on earth this adventure might take me. It certainly smelt very old; as if it had been closed up for a hundred years or more.

Yulia explained along the way that it was not in any way linked to the time tunnel. This passage was last used by a dog called Chilvester. He was alive during Victorian times and used to do good deeds in orphanages, workhouses and hospitals, helping humans and especially children whenever he could. He always travelled in secret and usually at night.

The passage was named after Chilvester and he lived a long and happy life. After his death the secret way had remained hidden and unused until this day. Only the guardian of the time tunnel and the woodland folk knew of its existence.

'You really are the Chosen One you know,' said Yulia, echoing Athelstan's words for the second time that night.

It wasn't a long journey but it was very dark and unfamiliar. The little lantern spluttered, casting just enough light to help us edge forward. We fell into companionable silence.

The cave-like ceiling dripped rusty smelling water which was cold and made me shiver when it hit my fur. I stopped and shook it off every now and then. Eventually we came to a dead end. We seemed to have come up against a solid wall.

'Have we taken a wrong turn?' I asked my guide.

'I can't remember what Athelstan said about how to exit the tunnel,' said Yulia, staring hard at the obstacle in front of us as if willing it to open and, when it didn't, she shook her head in frustration. I felt sure she was about to stamp her tiny foot so I shoved ahead with my nose which I had discovered was a very useful tool. The obstruction fell away with an alarming bang.

'Bravo!' shouted Yulia as she scuttled back down the passageway, the way we had just come.

'Okay I'll carry on from here then!' I said to Yulia's retreating back, trying to sound braver than I felt.

I was left wondering what to do next.

I put my paws on what seemed to be a ledge and peered out into the gloom; it certainly wasn't daylight, it was probably nightlight, for it was still dark. There was nothing else for it but to jump. Be brave and plunge into the unknown.

I counted to three and then quite gingerly, screwing my face up and bracing myself and then launched… and fell…just a few inches, landing four-square on my paws, in the fresh air.

The door closed behind me on an invisible hinge with a metallic thud and I could see a sign saying 'The Talbot Café' painted in gold.

Further investigation showed me that I was on the outside of a very old building. I glanced up and saw wide steps and columns leading up to the covered entrance. Moving down on to the pavement and looking up at the roof I could see a spire. Presumably this was a church. That made sense. It seemed that the Chilvester Passage ran from one church building to another. But where on earth was I and why had Athelstan wanted me to come here?

Chapter 6

Rolo finds Hope

The church stood on a road, on the edge of a square which had wide roads running all around it. A red bus went past with only one person on board. Then a black taxi cab with its orange light showing it was available for hire. Then another red bus. These were clues, I thought. Red buses, black cabs; I worked out that I was probably in London, but what year had I landed in?

I spied a road sign and went closer to read the black letters on its white rectangular background; the name of the road was Duncannon Street. I wondered again why I had been brought to London.

Something fluttering caught my eye and I saw a crumpled up newspaper blowing across the square, being chased by a street cleaner in the quieter hours of the capital city.

89

The Secret Adventures of Rolo

I chased it round a couple of fountains, pounced on it and held it down with my front paws so that the cleaner, plugged in to his music via headphones, could retrieve it and scoop it into his rubbish cart. This just gave me enough time to glance at the date on the top of the page; it showed today's date. So I hadn't time travelled then. I was still in the present.

The thought crossed my mind that this probably meant I wouldn't be able to communicate with anyone. Not that the street cleaner looked like he wanted to start a conversation with his headphones acting as a communication barrier.

He patted me and threw me a bit of burger from a discarded polystyrene take- away box before it joined the newspaper in the rubbish cart. I'm not proud when it comes to food, you know me, I'll eat anything, so I gobbled it up eagerly.

Here I was then, in Central London in the

middle of the night, without a clue as to where I should go.

An important man on a very tall column looked down at me as I pondered my dilemma. He was guarded by four lions on each corner. No wonder he looked so impressive.

I went back to the church and trotted up St Martin's Lane and then took a lottery of right turns and left turns and, after about twenty minutes, saw a pedestrian sign to a hospital.

I followed the direction it was pointing and eventually found myself outside a modern building and I walked under the canopy, drawn to an entrance painted in rainbow colours lit up by bright lights from within, despite the lateness of the hour.

This was a children's hospital. It seemed quite welcoming. I felt compelled to go in.

Being small, I easily avoided detection at the

front desk. The night time receptionist was engrossed in something on her smart phone. I trotted right past the desk well below eye level.

Thinking I wouldn't be able to reach the buttons in the lift and not too sure where I was heading, I thought I would take the stairs. There was no one in the stairwell, being past visiting time and all the parents and carers had gone home to rest. Only the night staff were moving silently within, quietly administering their care.

I was out of breath when I reached the fourth floor so I thought I'd have a look around there.

The heavy door from the stair well pushed open with a swoosh which momentarily disturbed the silence within. I held my breath. No one came. The silence was only punctuated by the occasional bleep of a machine.

Now as you know, I don't like high pitched noises, they make me bark, but I knew that these machines were doing an important job of saving sick children so I took the manly decision to try to keep my ears closed to the sound and try to blot it out. Definitely no barking.

The first thing I saw in a side ward were brightly coloured curtains decorated with cute puppies… pulled tightly closed around a bed. Further investigation (well, okay, I shoved my head through the join in the curtains) showed that the occupant of the bed was a pretty little girl fast asleep with her arm propped around a teddy.

She didn't look as if she should be in hospital at all. Her hair curled softly around her face and sprawled out like a spider across the pillow. It was a little damp where it touched her forehead. Her eyes were closed but I bet underneath the lids they were sky blue. Then I noticed the tubes and wires attached to this little poppet. The sleep was perhaps not so peaceful but necessary for healing.

I could hear someone coming and ducked underneath her bed where I was soon joined by the discarded teddy who landed face down with a soft plop beside me on the recently mopped disinfectant-smelling tiled floor. I cocked up an ear and listened.

Two night sisters were having a murmured conversation in low tones on the other side of the curtains about a little girl called Hope who had been in hospital for two weeks following an accident, and the doctors were puzzled as to why she was still in a coma and trying to think of ways her family could possibly encourage her to regain consciousness.

My instincts told me that her little body had shut down as part of the healing process and I'm sure the medical staff knew that.

One of the sisters bent down and I saw a

hand coming towards me under the bed. I pushed the discarded bear out with my front paw.

Phew that was close!

The hand picked up the bear and tucked it back into the bed covers next to the sleeping child. I listened to their muffled retreating footsteps as they moved along the corridor in their sensible shoes, tucking in strayed teddies and smoothing down beds on their rounds.

When all was quiet once more in the ward and the sisters had departed, I hopped up onto Hope's bed, nudged the bear back on the floor with a muttered apology and snuggled into the little girl's side, just the same as I did sometimes in the mornings with the floppy haired boy when the stair gate was open. I was very careful not to disturb the wires and tubes.

Hope stirred a little and her breathing

returned to its regular pattern. I snuggled in closer, hoping my live little furry body would somehow comfort her in a way that perhaps the static bear couldn't.

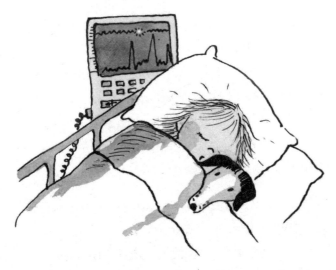

We lay peacefully like this for hours, Hope and I, with me keeping watch. The steady rhythmic bleep of her machines monitoring her every breath.

As the sun crept around the blackout blind, I roused myself from this comfortable position. The ward was starting to stir and soon there would be a flurry of hospital activity with the change of the night shift and the admittance of visitors after the rounds of the medical staff. I knew, much as I didn't want to leave this little girl's side, I would have to find my way back home and into my basket pretty sharpish before the smiley lady awoke and I was missed.

I jumped down off the bed and, as an afterthought, picked up the poor bear and tucked it back into the warm spot which I had just vacated next to Hope.

The London streets were coming to life and I knew I had to move quickly.

I found my way down tree-lined avenues and busy roads with names which flashed past in a blur. Names like 'Holborn', 'Bloomsbury Way', 'Monmouth Street' and at last the familiar 'St Martin's Lane' and there I saw the important man with his back to me, the lions still sitting alert, and the pigeons just arriving for their daily begging.

I scampered round the railings to The Talbot
Café sign and wondered what I had to do
to open the Chilvester Passage from the
London end. I sniffed around the bottom
of the sign and nudged it upwards with
my nose, and miraculously it opened, just
enough to squeeze my head and then my
shoulders through the gap.

I edged the rest of my body through and
dropped into the darkness of the passage on
the other side. I heard the board bang down
into place behind me and looked around for
my tiny lamp bearer. I needn't have worried.

She was there waiting for me.

'Well, Paddy Paws, you're later than I expected…did you work out what you had to do?' she asked as she hurried me along the dark passage.

'I found Hope who looked like she needed some companionship,' I replied wearily, and longed for my basket.

I left Yulia standing in the tunnel behind the dog mural and once more skittered across the tiled floor to the west door of the church.

It was still dark outside. I glanced up at the church clock and it said it was just before seven. Plenty of time to get home and into my basket before anyone in the house stirred. I was thankful for long winter nights and snuggled down in my bed, worrying about the little girl.

My next opportunity to visit Hope came sooner than expected.

The following evening, the smiley lady and floppy haired boy were going out to dinner with friends who owned cats, so they put me to bed much earlier than usual. Of course I didn't object, although they kept apologising and promised me treats upon their return.

As soon as I heard the car exit the drive, I knew the coast was clear. It would have been helpful if they had given me a lift into town but of course they didn't know that!

The main door of the church was open because there were a couple of people setting up seating for an evening concert. I strolled in unseen and then skirted the inside of the church walls keeping in the shadows and hiding behind the grand piano until the men had finished arranging the chairs for the expected audience.

I approached the dog mural and felt the same anticipation and frisson of excitement as I had felt the previous time. However, the edges did not blur and the door did not open.

I didn't know what to do. I ducked into the Lady Chapel as the shifters were about to move the grand piano into concert position. I was bitterly disappointed.

There was nothing else for it but to go home.

I slept for a while in my basket and dreamt of barrels.

A few hours later, my people came home, patted me, fed me with a bit of steak fat saved from their meal, and went upstairs to bed.

Yulia and the owl tapped on the window.

'Yulia!' I mouthed through the glass, 'Why wouldn't the Chilvester Passage open? What is it that I need? Is it the pink ball? I tried to return to see Hope this evening!'

'Ah sorry, Paddy Paws, I forgot to tell you, the Chilvester Passage only opens when the clock strikes twelve. Come, Athelstan needs you; a local adventure tonight; you're off to Devizes!'

I put a brave face on and pushed Hope to the back of my mind for now and opened the kitchen cupboard under the sink, moving the bottles and bucket to reveal the trapdoor.

Chapter 7

Rolo and the Moonrakers

I had visited Devizes several times with the smiley lady and I knew the Wadworth shire horses because I'd delivered a message to them on a previous adventure.

On this occasion, however, the time tunnel brought me out at the side of St James' church, next to the pond known as The Crammer.

I had no idea which century I was in this time, and started looking for clues. I couldn't see any sign of the big supermarket or even any cars. Wait a minute; there wasn't even a proper road, more of a cart track.

What **was** evident was that it was very late at night; the full moon shone brightly, illuminating the scene. I think it's what's referred to as a 'hunter's moon.'

At first glance there were not many people

around. Not surprising due to the lateness of the hour, but then I spied a flurry of activity around the pond. I edged a bit closer and hid behind a cart which was covered with heavy oilskin cloths.

Closer inspection revealed that men and women in dark clothes were pulling up barrels from a trapdoor and putting them in the pond. The barrels bobbed about for a few minutes on the surface, and then the men, using a variety of long handled farming implements, started fishing the barrels back out. I had no idea what they were up to.

'Psst.' I turned and saw some kind of Spaniel beside me. He leant towards me and asked in a whispered tone, 'Are you with the excise men?' I had no idea what he meant so I shook my head.

'Good. The name's Tubbs. Mister Tubbs to you.'

We sniffed each other politely and I avoided

eye contact with him as I didn't want to fight and certainly didn't feel like deferring to him.

'What are they doing?' I asked as casually as I could.

'They're hiding the brandy,' replied Tubbs. 'Or to be more precise, watering down the brandy.' He gave me a conspiratorial wink.

'Oh dear! Here comes trouble! Are you sure you're not with the excise men? 'The day has eyes but the night has ears,' he said, and when I looked puzzled he tapped the side of his nose and said it was an old Scottish proverb.

I assured him I wasn't with any excise men, whatever they were, and following him, I crawled under the cart and hid underneath the tarpaulin.

'Watch this,' said Tubbs. I put my head between my paws and peered out through a gap. 'Someone must have tipped them off. Sure it wasn't you?'

Some very officious looking men rode up at speed, dismounted their horses and demanded that everyone stopped what they were doing at once and put their tools down in the name of the King. The trapdoor had mysteriously closed.

'Which King would that be?' I casually whispered to my fellow fugitive.

'Why, George lll of course – did you just get off a tea clipper?' Tubbs hissed, no doubt puzzled by my ignorance.

I thought I'd better be quiet and observe what was going on.

'What are you fellows doing at this late hour, as if we didn't know?' demanded the man in charge, sporting a swirling cloak and big menacing sword.

One of the sharpest of the villagers pointed

at the moon's round yellow reflection in the pond and said loudly, 'We're trying to catch yonder cheese.'

The men of Devizes picked up their rakes and demonstrated how they were using their rakes to catch the moon, stroking at the surface of the water.

The excise men thought they had a right bunch of simpletons here; these villagers were thought to be a few shillings short of a guinea throughout the county, so they laughed amongst themselves and mounted their horses and rode off into the night, no doubt to try to surprise some other smugglers engaged in nocturnal activities. No cause for concern in Devizes then.

When the coast was clear, the villagers resumed their 'moon raking' and brought up barrel after barrel of fine French brandy, roped together and now slightly watered down by a dip in the Crammer but diluted to a strength that would be more palatable to the English taste and less likely to be detected as 'smuggled spirit' in local inns at the point of sale.

I asked Tubbs where the trapdoor led, and he said there was a secret passageway running underneath the marketplace in the town out to the Crammer. I was also curious about his name.

Tubbs explained he was born in a tubb which was another name for a small barrel. He

The Secret Adventures of Rolo

further enlightened me about smuggling, explaining that, owing to high taxation on luxury goods in Britain, many villagers all over the country had turned to illegal means of importing tobacco, tea and brandy.

This particular hoard was a consignment of French brandy, brought across the Channel by ship and then driven inland by horse and cart for local distribution and hidden in passageways and even the pond.

The price of brandy in France was a quarter of the price of a barrel in England. Former English governments had made themselves unpopular by putting taxes up higher and higher in order to pay for expensive wars in Europe and that was why many ordinary English folk became involved in smuggling in the first place. Hard working men simply couldn't afford life's little luxuries and thought the high taxation grossly unfair.

Tubbs also told me that tobacco was often disguised by twisting it into ropes to avoid detection by excise men as you would expect to find numerous coils of rope lying on the deck of a ship!

The excise men rode around the country looking for night-time activity which usually meant illegal imports and the rounding up of villagers who dodged paying their taxes. They had certainly been fooled in Devizes that night!

Tubbs gave me a small barrel with a rope tied to it and I looped it around my neck. I would take it back to Athelstan as a souvenir of my smuggling adventure.

The Secret Adventures of Rolo

I thought he would probably give it to Da; the woodland man looked as if he might enjoy a tiny drop of 18th century brandy. I felt a bit like a Saint Bernard dog about to go on a mountain rescue and thanked the spaniel. I was soon on my way back through the time tunnel to the foxhole entrance but instead of going straight home, I went through the forest to see Athelstan.

He seemed to be sleeping and awoke with a start.

'I didn't expect to see you tonight, Little Pup,' he yawned.

I told him about my adventure and asked him about smuggling, as I found it quite fascinating and wondered when it all came to an end. The wise gatekeeper enlightened me:

'The outbreak of the Napoleonic Wars brought a halt to most smuggling activity because the trading nations England and

France were suddenly at war, and then in 1840 a Free Trade policy was introduced in Britain which lowered taxes and so there was no longer a need to smuggle goods.'

Athelstan's encyclopaedic knowledge never failed to impress me – was there anything this guardian didn't know? I wondered.

I recounted my adventure and he listened, nodding wisely. I gave him the small barrel and told him that I now knew why the good people of Devizes were called 'moonrakers'.

I scampered home and under the rickety gate, up the garden steps. I'm sure I could hear the rabbits next door but no time to investigate now. I snuck through the trapdoor, scattering bottles onto the kitchen floor as I jumped out from the cupboard under the sink.

I quickly tidied up and then snuggled into my basket. I needn't have worried too much; being winter I had a few extra hours

112

of adventure time, as the sun had early nights and a lie in at this time of year and, thankfully, so did the smiley lady.

Dog Blog #3 - According to Rolo

The smiley lady is quite nervous driving in the countryside at this time of year because she is scared of 'brown eyes in the hedge'.

This is because it's the time of year when the young male deer go a bit silly. They make an extraordinary barking noise when they are rutting (which means they are testing their newly grown velvet antlers by running at each other and head butting). Sounds a bit daft to me.

That's why, if you are driving at night and pick up eyes reflected in the hedgerow, it means there is

usually at least one and probably
several deer about to spring out
in front of you and dent your car!
This also happens in spring time.

By the way, I heard a bang-bang-
banging in the garden and barked
so much I was shut inside the
house with the curtains drawn so
I couldn't see what was going on,
but later inspection revealed a new
fence.

The neighbours rabbits are once
more out of sight.

Chapter 8

Hope Revisited

The next night no winged messenger came a-tapping so I decided to wait until midnight and then try the Chilvester Passage again. It had been two days since I had met Hope and I really wanted to see how she was and how her recovery was progressing. I really wanted to see those eyes open to see if they were blue.

I reached the church at five to twelve and saw that the High Street was deserted. I entered the church under the west door, shoving the loose plank again, and stood in front of the dog mural, listening for the chimes.

Exactly as it happened the first time, the outline of the dog blurred and I found myself once again staring into the gaping hole. I didn't hesitate this time, however, and jumped straight in.

'How did you know I'd be here?' I asked the unmistakable silhouette of Yulia, as she struggled to light her lantern.

'Athelstan sent me,' she replied simply, as if that explained everything. Once more I found myself in awe of the guardian of the time tunnel and keeper of the forest and his ability to 'know'.

I used the same means as before (i.e. my nose) to open 'The Talbot Café' sign and exit the Chilvester Passage and just managed to jump clear before it shut fast behind me, almost catching my tail.

Luckily the square was just as deserted as my last visit.

I was born with an excellent sense of direction, although this time I took a slightly different route to the children's hospital.

I trotted up St Martin's Lane to Shaftesbury Avenue, then ran along Vernon Place, found

Theobalds Road, turned left into Boswell Street, and at Queen Square turned right into Great Ormond Street. The hospital building loomed ahead of me and I was drawn again towards the bold coloured stripes and bright lights of the entrance and noticed a statue of Peter Pan on the left as I entered through the main door. I kept a low profile, skirting the walls to avoid detection.

I needn't have worried; the same receptionist was still playing with her phone, although I did notice a couple of security cameras swivel round and follow me.

The security guard on duty at the time could not believe his eyes when he saw a little Jack Russell trotting through the hospital entrance on the CCTV monitor. He was sure that this was the same little dog he had seen a couple of nights earlier who disappeared from sight once he entered the stairwell. The security guard called his boss and instigated a search party to find the dog who entered the hospital without his owner.

Scampering up the stairs two at a time, I quickly found Hope on the fourth floor. Cute puppy curtains still firmly drawn. Glancing around at the dials on the machines and the squiggles on the charts there didn't seem to be any change in the condition of the young patient. She looked exactly the same to me and I doubted she had moved at all. She seemed to have been asleep forever, a bit like a modern-day blonde version of Snow White.

Without further ado, I kicked the teddy out of bed and snuggled under the blankets into Hope's side.

I held my breath under the blankets when I heard the gruff voice of a man asking the night sister if she'd seen a little dog anywhere on the ward. She replied that she hadn't and the man went away. I relaxed.

I was sure I felt Hope's little body move

to accommodate me and I responded by snuggling right in. I licked the pale frail arm which was lying on top of the covers, and I'm certain I felt a flicker of response. Maybe I was imagining it because I really wanted it to happen.

We lay like this for several hours, only disturbed by the rounds of the night staff keeping an eye on the sleeping patients and the occasional flash of a torch as the heavy booted security man continued his search for an evasive little dog that kept appearing on the monitor over a succession of nights. I had to keep my wits about me and an ear up to avoid detection.

Once again I hid under the bed as soft footsteps approached the puppy curtains.

I lifted an ear and heard them saying in hushed tones that Hope's parents were very worried that nothing familiar seemed to be able to bring her out of the coma and that it had been more than two weeks now: not her teddy nor her favourite music or even stories read aloud by familiar voices. They were at their wits end and praying for a miracle. Hope was breaking hearts.

I resumed my position, snuggled into the little girl's side, and, just before dawn broke, I spotted a tape recorder on the night stand and it gave me an idea. I jumped down, replaced the long suffering bear and sneaked out of the curtains, leaving as discreetly as I had come, trying my best not to be detected and leaving the security man in the control room scratching his head in puzzlement.

The next night when I visited, I definitely felt Hope respond when I snuggled in, and then, when I licked her face, I believe I saw her eyelids flicker and the merest hint of a smile on those rosebud lips.

These visits continued regularly for the next few nights, with Hope becoming more and more responsive whenever I was at her side. Frustrating to have to wait until midnight to use the Chilvester Passage, though, as it only gave me a few hours.

On the last night, as I snuggled towards her warm body, she opened her eyes and stared directly at me. I was right; those peepers were as blue as cornflowers.

The machines suddenly made a different sound altogether and I could hear footsteps approaching at a pace. Perhaps the monitors had registered the fact that Hope had regained consciousness. 'Time to act quickly Rolo, make like a tree and leave,' I thought to myself.

The next day I was in the forest with the smiley lady, off the lead and running freely, pretending to chase a squirrel, and I had the chance to go and have a word with Athelstan. Something was troubling me;

'You know the Chilvester Passage only opens when the clock strikes twelve? Well what would happen if I found a way to record the clock chimes and play them so I could use the Passage at a different time of day, would that work?'

'Well now, you'll just have to try it and see, Little Pup,' the guardian smiled.

Seeing the tape recorder in the hospital had given me the idea. I knew that somewhere in the mess of the box room there was an old cassette recorder which the smiley lady used to use to record her singing practice to help her to learn her choir songs, in the days before she had a smart phone.

All I had to do was find it. Whilst the floppy haired boy was stretched out watching television and the smiley lady was pottering in the garden admiring the new growth, I ran upstairs. Luckily the box room door was slightly ajar and I only had to push it.

The room was full of boxes of junk; all kinds of stuff saved by the smiley lady over the years: school books from her three children,

certificates, photographs, programmes from
concerts and theatre. Where on earth to
start? I spied a box which said 'music' and
tipped it up and out fell a jumble of song
sheets, and the sought after tape recorder.
No time to tidy the box; I had to stow the
tape recorder safely somewhere before it was
discovered.

Unfortunately the box room door had not
been hung on the level, and it had swung
closed behind me. I was trapped inside
the smallest room with the item I so badly
needed!

I could hear the smiley lady coming up the
stairs calling me. Perhaps she thought I was
playing hide and seek. I heard her opening
every door and finally the box room door
flew open.

I was ready; had my head down so she
couldn't see what I carried in my mouth, and
charged into the floppy haired boy's room
next door, shoving the tape recorder under

his bed. It was such a mess in there, he'd never notice it!

The smiley lady shooed me back downstairs and went back out into the garden. The floppy haired boy hadn't moved an inch so I raced back upstairs, picked up the tape recorder in my teeth and brought it downstairs and hid it under the cushion in my doggy bed. Phew! I think I got away with it.

That night, when my people had gone to bed, I fiddled with the buttons on the tape recorder. Luckily the batteries were still working otherwise that might have been another challenge!

A horrid screeching noise came out from the tape recorder – I could only assume it was the smiley lady singing at the top of her voice but the song was completely unrecognisable, whatever it was.

I pressed 'stop' pretty sharpish as I didn't

The Secret Adventures of Rolo

want to wake the house up. Further investigation showed that the red button was for 'record'. I waited for Yulia and the owl to come tapping, and I explained through the window what I needed them to do, and how to operate the machine, pressing 'record' and 'play' at the same time and I rewound the tape to the beginning.

Yulia confirmed she understood and would do this for me, but she said that Athelstan had a mission for me. She thought that Da could light the way for me through the time tunnel but I told her not to worry; if she lent me her lantern I could carry it carefully and leave it in the time tunnel for my return.

She could then use Da's lantern and go with the owl to record the chimes of the clock at midnight. I gave her the tape recorder and said it would be useful if she could hide it in the Lady Chapel at the church. Then it would be in place ready for my next opportunity to use the Chilvester Passage.

125

Yulia gave me Athelstan's vague instructions: to enter the time tunnel and see where it took me. My mission would become evident. Very mysterious indeed!

I was just about to enter the foxhole tunnel entrance when I was set upon, thankfully not by a lion dog or a wolf but by Chickpea!

'What have you been up to Rolo? Haven't seen you for ages!' she said excitedly as we righted ourselves.

I told her I'd been busy but didn't give away the secret of the Chilvester Passage.

'I left the pink ball here under the bushes look!' said Chickpea, very pleased with herself. I told her off, as it occurred to me that any dog might be able to enter the time tunnel with a pink ball and we couldn't have that, could we? Imagine if the Dalmation, or a Labrador or any other number of dogs went time travelling. Thankfully they were all way too big to fit.

The Secret Adventures of Rolo

Dog Blog #4   - According to Rolo

This morning the smiley lady woke me up at 7am — this is half an hour earlier than usual! We went out almost straightaway for walkies over the fields.

Too early to see any other dogs.

After breakfast I was bundled in the car and we drove to Chippenham which is about 18 miles away, for a school visit. I know the routine — it's where I get to sit in the car for a short while and then I get a long walk after. It's another sunny day so the smiley lady parked in the shade and left me with all the windows open and a bowl of water. Actually between you and me she left the car unlocked because I have worked out how to set off the car alarm by jumping around and it's the only way she can disable the alarm!

I slept for about 40 minutes and dreamt about a shiny trophy and then a lovely blonde bubbly lady in a pretty dress came to the car and took me into school! She walked me right into the KS1 hall where the smiley lady was talking about my book and showing my pictures on a big screen!

Having me walk in at that moment threw her a bit but after I'd kissed her enthusiastically I sat nicely with my new friend and listened. She's not too bad really, she seems to know my book pretty well, but then she did type it! She'd lost her audience, though, as they were all thoroughly distracted

by my appearance. Yes I know I'm
cute.

After the presentation, some Year 6
children came to help us pack away
and they made a big fuss of me. The
rest of KS2 were pretty jealous
they didn't get to see me! It was
great way to start off King's Lodge
School's book week — I am such a
famous rescue dog!

Chapter 9

Rolo and the World Cup Theft

Carrying Yulia's tiny lantern carefully by its handle in my front teeth, Chickpea and I made slow progress through the time tunnel.

As we exited, I sniffed the air and looked around to see where we could possibly be this time. I left the lamp inside the tunnel. Where were we? I looked around for clues.

We came blinking into the sunshine in the middle of a busy square with traffic going round on all sides. I could see three black

The Secret Adventures of Rolo

lions on identical plinths to the one we had just climbed out from, and a tall column in the middle of the square with an important man perched on the top. I knew exactly where we were and only a short distance from the Chilvester Passage!

The cars looked old fashioned and, judging by the look of the red buses and the number plates and the short skirts being worn by ladies with big hairdos, I reckoned we were in the 1960s.

For some inexplicable reason I felt the urge to jump on a bus and of course Chickpea followed. We sneaked under an itchy checkered-cushion bench seat, unseen by the conductor who was wearing a peaked cap and whistling whilst he was leaning on a floor to ceiling pole in the gap at the back of the bus. The bus conductor was almost hanging out in the road as he swung around the pole and I thought he might be showing off. He had a fascinating silver

131

machine hanging around his neck on a wide strap, and the machine made an interesting whizzing noise when he clicked some dials and turned the handle. Then it spat out long white paper tickets which he tore off with a flourish as he strode along the lower deck, talking cheerily to the passengers and greeting most of them by name.

We didn't have any money and I wasn't sure if we needed a ticket so we stayed hidden, eyed suspiciously by a black Scottie dog sitting very primly on its owner's lap.

When I saw Big Ben and the Houses of Parliament, I was pleased to see a lady reach up and pull the cord that set the bell ringing to warn the bus driver up the front to stop, as this was a request stop. I had a strong feeling that we had to get off the bus in Westminster but I couldn't tell you why.

We snuck off the bus, hidden behind a shopper's wicker basket.

According to Big Ben's unmistakable round clock face, it was late afternoon.

Now what? Right next to the bus stop I saw a sign on a building saying 'Methodist Central Hall'. I stood up on my hind legs and peered through the window. We Jack Russells are nothing if not curious!

A small poster was advertising the fact that the famous golden Jules Rimet Trophy was being exhibited alongside a rare stamp collection, three months ahead of the World Cup finals being played in the capital.

The Secret Adventures of Rolo

'I'd love to have a closer look at the World Cup! I hear it's made of solid gold and worth a fortune!' whispered Chickpea.

I hadn't worked out what we were actually in London for, so we trotted up the stone steps, spun round in the revolving door and somehow got inside hidden amongst the creased trouser legs and shiny city shoes flocking into the building for a glimpse of the trophy.

'You'll have to be quick ladies and gents, it's almost closing time!' said a man officiously jangling a bunch of keys on a big hoop.

We ducked under one of the glass topped frames that contained sheets of postage stamps. Men sporting trilby hats with either mackintoshes over their arms or folded newspapers tucked under them, and umbrellas hooked over them, bent over the glass and stared intently at the contents. Most of them seemed to be wearing the same style thick, black, square-framed glasses.

Across the room a small crowd gathered
in awe around a glass case containing the
gleaming golden trophy; the most famous
and sought after prize in football, the Jules
Rimet.

A bell rang and a voice announced that it
was closing time.

A black felt cover was draped heavily over
the display case we were hiding under, right
down to the floor.

'Who put the lights out?' squeaked Chickpea
in alarm.

'Now what, smartypaws?' she asked as
we peered out through a slit in the cloth,
watching all the dark suits and short skirts
departing through the doors as if someone
had pulled the bath plug out.

A few moments later we heard the click
of the key in the lock and the room was
plunged into darkness leaving behind the

smell of Old Spice aftershave hanging in the air.

'We have to get back to the time tunnel!' wailed Chickpea. 'My people will be very upset if they find my basket empty!'

I was getting a bit fed up with her whining. 'I didn't ask you to come with me,' I snapped. 'You just invited yourself!'

Then, seeing her little crestfallen face I added more kindly, 'Don't worry, we can always get back home; we just need to work out how we get out of this building.'

Both of us made a thorough investigation of the exhibition hall and were trying not to give in to despair. It looked as if we might have to stay until morning when presumably the door would be unlocked. We slept for a few hours, lost in our own thoughts, and then we heard a loud noise. It sounded like someone was outside trying to come in, but not through the door. We instinctively hid under the heavy cover again.

There was the sound of the swinging of a hefty sledge hammer or something similar and that was followed at once by the tinkling of breaking glass. I braced myself, waiting for the inevitable sound of a security alarm going off. (You know how I hate those.)

Amazingly, though, all remained silent. The sensors were attached to the front of the trophy display case, not the back which was up against the wall and now sported a man-sized hole visible in the flash of a torch beam.

I peeped out from under the cover and saw a pair of very shiny brown pointed shoes as they appeared in the hole behind the case, which now left the famous trophy standing unprotected and highly vulnerable.

I watched, mesmerised as I witnessed gloved hands remove the golden cup through the hole in the wall and stuff the precious trophy inside a cloth sack.

137

The Secret Adventures of Rolo

The lid fell, and I thought it would clang an alarm, but the man caught it with his free hand and stuffed it, too, into the sack which he bundled up and slid inside his jacket.

I couldn't get a look at the thief's face as he had a trilby pulled down and his features were in shadow, but his jaws were working; he seemed to be chewing something, and I registered to memory the shiny brown pointed shoes. He spat something into a piece of paper from his pocket and I saw him screw it up and drop it on the floor.

The thief's work was done and silent as night he exited the way he had entered; through the back of the exhibition hall, and that gave us the escape route we trapped dogs desperately needed.

I stopped to investigate what he had dropped on the floor. I sniffed at it. It smelt of spearmint and was screwed up tightly in a ball wrapped in a slip of paper. The discarded gum was still sticky so I carefully peeled

The Secret Adventures of Rolo

off the paper and memorised the printed address. I then screwed it all up together and kicked it under the wooden bench with my now very sticky spearminty front paw. Eeuuw! Horrid stuff!

The hole in the wall that the burglar had made led us into an adjoining church and we followed in his footsteps as, in his haste, he had left the exit door slightly open.

We needed to get back to Trafalgar Square pretty quick. I saw a black taxi cab with the yellow light on and the driver snatching forty winks at the wheel of his taxi whilst waiting for his next passenger. The back door had been left open by the previous fare and, as luck would have it, a call came through for a pick-up at Charing Cross station.

'Quick, follow me,' I barked at Chickpea. For once she held her tongue. We had a free ride and jumped out unseen at the mainline station, just a stone's throw away from Trafalgar Square and the time tunnel entrance.

Now this is where I have to confess I messed up. I am normally a fairly intelligent Jack Russell, but I am used to operating solo. I forgot all about my wingman Chickpea. She was lagging behind a bit and peering in shop windows and I crossed the road to the square without waiting for her.

I found the right lion statue and opened the trapdoor in the plinth and jumped straight into the time tunnel. It was pitch black.

I was looking for Yulia and had forgotten my manners, and didn't hold the door open for Chickpea. It shut with a resounding bang behind me. Then I remembered that Yulia was away on my recording mission and so I went off, homeward bound, using Yulia's lantern that I'd left inside the tunnel.

It wasn't until I reached the foxhole that I realised I had left my companion behind in London in the Swinging Sixties! I didn't know what to do, but assumed Chickpea would eventually follow. I had to get back to my bed as I was running out of time.

I ran up the hill hoping not to be seen. I needn't have worried. It was still pitch dark and very cold. Even the sun hadn't got up yet.

I crept into my basket and crawled under the blanket. I was exhausted from the exhilaration of the adventure but couldn't sleep much because I was thinking about my abandoned companion and wondering if she'd found the right lion plinth and indeed if she'd managed to get home safely, otherwise she would be stuck in 1966!

Early next morning, out for walkies on the field, we saw Chickpea's owners looking very agitated indeed. They were calling and calling for her. I was hoping against hope to be flattened at any moment by a small energetic Jack Russell, but of course Chickpea was nowhere to be seen. When the smiley lady questioned her absence, Chickpea's owners explained that she hadn't been seen since yesterday evening. The smiley lady made sympathetic noises and told them not to worry as we would keep our eyes open for the missing dog.

'No good searching the fields, smiley lady, I know exactly where she is,' I thought to myself, but of course I couldn't say anything out loud. I did the next best thing and went into Eeyore mode (which meant I sat down and dug my heels in, dragging on the lead) and the smiley lady eventually took the hint, cut my walk short and we went home early. She said I looked a bit sheepish.

'You're definitely out of sorts, Rolo. I'll have to leave you alone in the house for a while; be a good boy. I have to go out for a while,' she said, picking up her car keys. I was glad that she talked to me like a human. I glanced at the front door; the skate board was missing so I assumed that the floppy haired

The Secret Adventures of Rolo

boy was also out. I would have to seize the moment.

I picked up the pink ball and raced to the foxhole entrance of the time tunnel. No time to waste. No time to find Yulia either. Powering on in the dark tunnel, guilt overwhelmed me. Emerging from the base of the lion plinth I spotted Chickpea at once, chasing pigeons round the fountains in the shadow of Nelson's Column. Some girls with short skirts and beehive hair do's gathered round stroking her.

'She's shivering,' said one in a yellow polka dot dress. Actually it's the terrier shake, but I didn't say anything.

'Oh, look, there's another one.' Oh no! I'd been spotted.

'Look, he's matching!'

'Sweet.'

'Come here, poppet.' Next thing I knew we

were being lifted up and told to 'say cheese' whilst one of the girls pressed a button on a big camera she wore around her neck. The camera made an alarming swooshing sound and a square picture shot out. She held it up. It looked blank to me. Then she flapped it around in the air and miraculously a picture started appearing of Chickpea and me and a bunch of strangers. After smothering us with cherry-red lipstick kisses and choking us with a cloud of Yves Saint Laurent Rive Gauche perfume, they at last put us down on the pavement.

Chapter 10

Forgiveness and Restoration

'Thank goodness!' I exclaimed, greeting Chickpea with my wet nose. 'I'm so sorry. Are you hungry?' She turned away. Oh dear, I was getting the silent treatment. We trotted off across the square, making a quick escape from the giggly girls and their Polaroid camera.

'Actually I'm starving!' she replied with a weak smile, and I led the way round the corner to a hamburger joint called Wimpy where I thought we could scavenge some scraps for my poor little friend. We were in luck. The bin was overflowing with uneaten fast food, and I saw a sign which read rather ironically, 'Keep Britain Tidy'.

'Didn't you remember where the time tunnel entrance was?' I asked Chickpea as she wolfed down half a discarded burger.

'No, I couldn't think exactly where we had come out. I thought it best to wait in Trafalgar Square when I realised I had lost you. I thought it was one of the four lions but I couldn't remember which one and none of them seemed to have a visible trapdoor. I can't believe you just left me in London!'

I made my apologies again. After food, I think she softened a bit. Never argue with a hungry woman.

'We have to get you home as soon as possible; your people are out looking for you,' I said, anxiously.

'I've stayed out a couple of times before so I don't think they will be too concerned but I've never been away for quite this long. Come on, I've had quite enough of London,' she replied, with a French fry hanging unattractively out of her mouth.

We found the time tunnel entrance at the base of the lion plinth in Trafalgar Square.

Chickpea and I found our way home in silence. I didn't really know what to say to her. We were relieved to see daylight through the foxhole entrance and knew it was early afternoon. We crossed the road, scampered up the hill and ran into the field.

'Chickpea, there you are! Where have you been?' The little dog was immediately scooped up by her lycra clad dad who had been out for a run, and carried home for inspection by his anxious children. 'Chickpea's home!' I heard them chorus as the front door shut with a bang. I heard the cat flap rattle, echoing its annoyance with me.

Unobserved, I ran home and just managed to get through the trapdoor and tidy the bottles under the sink before I heard a car engine and the smiley lady and floppy haired boy came in noisily through the front door. She was telling him not to leave his skateboard where people could trip over it. I greeted

147

them in the usual fashion, jumping up and nipping their fingers so they would not suspect anything was amiss. They were too busy looking for puddles.

I slept in my basket for most of the afternoon. I knew I'd have to return through the time tunnel to London that night as I had to pass on my information to the police dogs back in 1966. I was, after all, a very important witness to the theft of the World Cup trophy and I couldn't just let it rest.

But first I had something important to do, in present time. I had to go back to the hospital and see how Hope was progressing. That would involve using the Chilvester Passage. Well at least I would have a chance to test out the recorded chimes!

We were watching television. I overheard the smiley lady talking to the floppy haired boy whilst I was sat on her lap. She said that she was going to drop him at a friend's house and then she was going out so I would have to be put to bed early that evening, necessitating an early walk. It suited me just fine as I was anxious to see Hope.

The floppy haired boy threw a ball for me a few times over on the field and I chased it half-heartedly. I didn't want to wear myself out too much. I saw Chickpea on her lead. We didn't make eye contact.

As soon as the car had left the drive, I opened the cupboard door and knocked the bottles and bucket aside under the kitchen sink and then stopped in my tracks. A key was turning in the front door.

'Only me! Forgot my skateboard!' shouted the floppy haired boy. Thank goodness it was still in the hall, where it shouldn't be, otherwise I might have been caught in the act, emptying the kitchen cupboard!

The door banged shut behind him and I heard the key turn and the car pull away again. I climbed into the cupboard and twisted the ring to open the trapdoor. Phew, that was close!

I raced the local bus down to the High Street in broad daylight. There were quite a few people visiting the redundant church as there seemed to be a local art exhibition going on.

 I managed to sneak in through the front door behind some legs, quite unobserved and retrieve the tape recorder from where Yulia had hidden it in the Lady Chapel.

Masked by the loud chatter and clatter of cups and saucers in the coffee shop, as the people of Marlborough dissected the amateur paintings of local scenes and still life, I managed to softly play my recording of the twelve chimes, holding my breath in case anyone noticed a Jack Russell waving a tape recorder at the wall, underneath the grand piano.

Luck was with me. Amazingly, undetected, I entered the Chilvester Passage through the blurry outline of the dog on the wall. I turned off the tape recorder and left it just inside the entrance.

It was only late afternoon when I emerged through the Talbot Café sign in the shadow of St Martin in the Fields. I turned up St Martin's Lane and set off on my familiar journey, whichever route I chose. Thankfully there were a few trees scattered on street corners so it was possible to relieve myself.

 I noticed that the streets of London were a lot busier than usual, with traffic and pedestrians. Commuters all hurrying in the same direction towards Charing Cross station on a mission to get home from work; most had their heads down and their fingers or ears attached to their mobile phones and a general scrabble to pick up free newspapers from a box on the street corner to read on the train.

It suddenly occurred to me that I was much more visible in the daytime. Dogs did not roam freely in the streets of the capital! If only I could pop into the police station and have a word with the police dogs and make a statement I could kill two birds with one stone whilst I was here. How silly of me! Of course, I would have to travel back to 1966 to do that!

I followed my nose at quite a pace, dodging pedestrians and traffic and stopping occasionally to water the trees and before long I was outside the now familiar main entrance to the hospital.

I managed to hide in a porter's trolley and soon found myself wheeled inside the foyer and the trolley stopped, as luck would have it, very close to the door which led to the staircase whilst the porter signed in.

There were quite a few people in the hospital because it was still 'visiting time' and I had to keep my wits about me to avoid detection. Dogs were definitely not allowed in hospitals and I certainly didn't want that nosey security man picking me up on his CCTV camera again!

Reaching the fourth floor by means of the stairs, I was very concerned when I entered the ward and saw the puppy curtains open, Hope's bed empty and the sheets stripped off it. No sign of her at all. I feared the worst and my tail nearly hit the floor. Fortunately, I couldn't have been more wrong!

Keeping my ears open as I hid behind the overflowing waste paper bin in the nurse's station, I learned that Hope had made a sudden and miraculous recovery from her coma and that when she regained consciousness she kept on and on to her parents about the little angel dog that had been looking after her in the night time.

Her parents were baffled but extremely relieved, and they blamed the medication and thought their daughter had been imagining things. They were so delighted to have their precious Hope back they didn't take too much notice of her ramblings.

Hope kept talking about the angel dog like a stuck record and eventually her parents had to promise that they would take her to Dogs Trust to rescue a dog just as soon as she was well enough.

I listened to this conversation with a smile and was only sorry that I didn't have the opportunity to meet the little girl I had grown so fond of. I trotted down the corridor, tail high in the air.

'Mum, that's him! That's my angel dog!' I glanced back over my shoulder and saw Hope walking in between her parents, holding their hands. The bear was tucked under her dad's arm. 'Come on, Rolo! Time for a hasty exit.' I told myself as I broke into a trot.

Just at that moment the security guard shouted to his boss that the cheeky little dog was again visible on CCTV, currently on level 4, and I heard him over the walkie talkie asking whether he should arrange another search party or if they should just concentrate on finding out how he was getting in and out of the building.

As the staircase door closed behind me I heard Hope's dad promise her that they would find an angel dog at Dogs Trust, just like me. Well, not quite, I thought. I'm special. There's only one of me.

I overheard the crackly voice on the walkie talkie say to the vigilant security guard,

'There's a little girl called Hope on this floor who thinks she has been visited by an angel dog who has been aiding her recovery. The head of the hospital wonders if this angel dog could work some miracles on the other sick children in this hospital. Allow him free passage as he is clearly a very clever dog.'

Phew, that called him off then. I trotted out past Peter Pan with my head held high.

My work here was done. Hope had been restored. Quickly away from Great Ormond Street and back to The Talbot Café sign at St Martin in the Fields.

I had to keep my wits about me when crossing the busy roads, as cyclists get very cross when pedestrians dive in front of them instead of waiting for the sign of the green man indicating it is safe for them to cross the road. Sometimes I have to remember to act less like a dog and more like a human.

As I exited the Chilvester Passage in the redundant church and tucked the tape recorder away in the Lady Chapel for future use, I wondered whether I could reach any other churches in London or whether the passage only went from A to B. I must remember to ask Athelstan some time.

Yulia and Bubo the owl came to tell me some good news. The time tunnel entrance in the Athelstan tree was once again open. The woodland folk had accepted the help of the animals of the forest, and foxes, moles, rabbits and mice had helped clear the blocked passage under Da's supervision. Athelstan was delighted.

I approached the guardian of the time tunnel and he was very pleased to see me. I told him that I needed to return to 1966 London because I had witnessed the break in at the stamp exhibition which had led to the theft of the World Cup trophy.

'On you go then, little pup,' he smiled. 'Where's your friend Chickpea?'

'I wouldn't be surprised if her cat flap has been boarded up for a while!' I said.

I asked him about the Chilvester Passage and he just smiled his woody smile, which made me think I was yet to discover where else it might take me.

I dropped the pink ball in the tree roots and squeezed my way into the time tunnel

157

underneath the Athelstan tree, shaking off remaining bits of sawdust and twigs from the clean-up operation in the forest. Yulia was already there with her lantern.

Chapter 11

Rolo on the Case

Meanwhile back in Westminster in 1966 two months had passed and the police still had no clue as to the missing World Cup's whereabouts; only a few red herrings.

The London Metropolitan police were at their wits end and the newspapers were full of it. Made-up sightings of the cup and photographs of foreign suspects had been flocking into Scotland Yard from all over the world right from the minute the news of the theft leaked out.

It had all become a huge joke. London's finest crime solvers were being ridiculed because the cup had been stolen 'on their patch', as the headquarters of the Metropolitan Police was right next door to the scene of the crime.

The police were supposed to have been guarding the famous and valuable trophy at

The Secret Adventures of Rolo

the time of the incident. Would the World Cup competition itself now have to be cancelled? Would they have to make a fake trophy in secret? How would England look in the eyes of the world? No, something would have to be done, and pretty quick, to save the integrity of the great footballing nation!

Approaching New Scotland Yard I spotted a navy blue Commer police van parked outside on the pavement.

A team of constables and detectives could be seen through a first floor window, scratching their heads and thumbing through their notebooks in the incident room, going over all the leads they had in case they had missed a vital clue.

Two German Shepherd dogs were tied to the railings outside the van, waiting for their next instruction. One was known as Bullseye and the other was called Sniffer.

Sniffer seemed to be in charge. I had to be careful how I played this or I might find myself under suspicion!

I overhead Bullseye telling Sniffer that things were pretty desperate and that there would soon to be a line-up of suspects: passers-by would be asked to try to identify the thief from a bunch of men who were members of the public as well as a few known criminals. They were going to bring in a few witnesses, including the cleaner who had seen someone lurking around the cloakrooms of the exhibition hall on the afternoon in question.

Sniffer confessed that he wasn't too hopeful as there just wasn't anything to go on. He'd been on many identity parades before and it was going to be very difficult to pick out a suspect when they all looked the same. This line up would likely be no different with all the men wearing trilby hats pulled down over their faces, and their collars turned up. Their features were always in shadow. How would any one particular person stand out?

I gave a polite little cough and stepped out from the shadows.

'I believe I may have some information that may help you catch your thief,' I said as bravely as I could.

I had their full attention now, as they strained on their leashes to get a better look at me.

'What makes you think you can help?' asked Bullseye gruffly.

'Tell me, what do you police dogs do if you're at the scene of a crime and there is a tall fence in your way, blocking your vision?' I asked politely.

'Why, we put our paws up and peer over it of course – we are big dogs. It's part of our training!' replied Sniffer.

'Well, we little dogs look under the fence and

see things you probably don't even notice,' I
replied. I could see both police dogs thinking
about this and not really getting it.

'What are you trying to say, scruffy?'

I let that go.

'I think your man was wearing shiny brown
pointed shoes, and if I am not mistaken, he
chews Wrigley's spearmint gum. You'll find
the evidence you need under the big heavy
bench inside the exhibition hall on the right
of the empty trophy case…you might even
find the thief's address if you use a bit of
intelligence.'

'How on earth could you know that? Dogs
can't see in colour! Just a minute, we found
dog hair around the empty case at the scene
of the crime; how do we know you're not the
thief?' Bullseye barked suspiciously. Sniffer
raised an eyebrow.

'Trust me,' I said as mysteriously as I could,

163

and, as these big dogs were chained up and I wasn't, I took my leave of Sniffer of the Yard and Bullseye and legged it around the corner.

The comment about not seeing in colour puzzled me. I thought to myself they probably could only see in black and white because it was the 1960s. I put it to the back of my mind. Not important for now.

The dogs' angry barks soon brought policemen scurrying from the incident room and they quickly unleashed the dogs and piled into the back of the Commer van and put the blue flashing light on. The streets were filled with the sound of 'nee naw' as they screeched only a couple of hundred yards to the crime scene, arriving before they'd even shut the back door of the van.

I smiled to myself from my hiding place behind a dustbin, and then pondered the more immediate dilemma of where on earth the trophy might be? The World Cup finals were due to start in a month and still no sign of the stolen trophy. I could only hope it hadn't been melted down for its solid gold properties; surely it was too well-known to sell on. Hopefully the thief was still hiding it at home.

I remembered the address on the piece of paper that wrapped the discarded chewing gum. I went secretly by train, amongst the stowed bicycles in the guards van, from Charing Cross to Norwood in South London, and found the house. With my ear up against the window, I overheard a very nervous and heated exchange of ideas as to what to do with 'the package' and how to extort a hefty ransom. An argument ensued.

I went down the path and back onto the street, thinking the best course of action was to hide between two parked cars and wait and see what happened next. My instinct told me that the thief was panicking and losing his nerve. He would have to get rid of the package.

One car was a Ford Anglia and the other a Morris Traveller. I saw a man come out of the front door in question carrying a holdall. He stuffed a package wrapped in newspaper under the front wheel of the Anglia.

From where I was hiding I could smell the distinctive aroma of spearmint gum. The shifty looking man glanced around him and then scuttled back inside number 68.

A quick pawing of the newspaper under the wheel arch of the Anglia revealed the unmistakable gleam of gold and now I had to figure out what to do and how to draw the attention of the police.

I knew I couldn't go back to the police dogs so I had to stand guard over the Cup and just hope that the police dogs had led their masters to the clue I told them about, and that they had found the address and were now on their way to apprehend the man who smelt of spearmint.

A black and white Collie dog was approaching, on a lead. He bent down to greet me between the two cars, and his owner tugged on his lead. I saw a folded up newspaper under the man's arm with the headlines about the possible cancellation of the football competition.

I whispered to the Collie 'do you want to become famous?' He looked surprised.

'Show your owner that parcel under the wheel!' I whispered to the docile and obliging dog.

Just at that moment I heard the familiar 'nee naw' of the police van, and Bullseye and Sniffer flew out from the back doors the minute the vehicle came to a standstill and they dragged their police handlers up the path of number 68.

'Go on, now's your chance,' I whispered under my breath.

The Secret Adventures of Rolo

I stayed out of sight and watched the police lead a handcuffed man with shiny brown shoes down the front garden and push his head down as they bundled him into the back of the van. I was fairly sure I could smell the faint aroma of Wrigley's spearmint gum as they passed me.

The next thing I saw was the dog walker crouching in the gutter and exclaiming: 'I don't Adam and Eve it! Pickles 'ere has found the ruddy World Cup!'

Once more my mission was complete and it was time for a sharp exit.

Hitching another ride from Norwood to Charing Cross amongst the bicycles, I passed under the ticket barrier amongst bare legs, short skirts and sharp suits and crossed the road carefully, setting off in the direction of Trafalgar Square.

As I trotted along, I saw a blue police box. There were quite a few of them around in the 1960s but you don't see them anymore. I believe that the purpose of them was a telephone to the nearest police station.

I went a bit closer to have a look as I hadn't seen a police box at close range before. I lifted my leg on the corner and the box made a strange noise and disappeared. Definitely time to get back to the 21st century I thought. Maybe I wasn't the only one to be time travelling around here!

Chapter 12

Rolo and the Sphinx

Next time I saw Athelstan in the day time, whilst off my lead and scampering freely in the forest, I thought he looked a little bit distracted.

He explained what the problem was and gave me a 'present time' mission to accomplish.

'I'm terribly worried about the badgers. Have you heard that they are being culled as they are blamed for the spread of tuberculosis amongst cattle? There is a set nearby and I know that government officials are coming to exterminate all badgers in the area. Is there anything you can do to help?'

Here was the guardian of the forest giving me permission to preserve a badger set from human destruction! I realised I would have to be a bit careful as we Jack Russells are built with stocky arms which bend outwards from the elbow and can be the bane of our lives when digging as we sometimes get stuck and cannot reverse out from a hole.

I thought it would be better if I took a wingman on this expedition and wondered whether Chickpea's grounding had come to an end yet and it would also be a good excuse to invite her along to get back in her good books. That was my reasoning. I told Athelstan not to worry; that I would personally go down to the badgers' set and lead them all to safety.

As I ran back to the smiley lady on the other side of the bushes, I was pounced upon by my little friend and once I had righted myself I said that was funny as I'd just been thinking about her and was wondering if she could escape at night again.

'Yes, they've unlocked the cat flap because I keep on howling in the night to go out for a wee and my family like their sleep!' she replied with a smile.

The Secret Adventures of Rolo

I told her about the plight of the badgers and she was keen to help at once.

'I don't know when the officials are coming so we'd better do this as soon as we can,' I said.

'Are you thinking what I'm thinking?' asked Chickpea

'No time like the present' and, with that, we both tore off as fast as we could to the clearing, no doubt leaving our owners wondering where we'd run off to. Jack Russell owners do know that if two or more get together, they tend to just run about and let off steam, so I didn't think they would be too worried.

'I'll go first,' I shouted back to Chickpea as we entered the badger set. 'Watch my back as I don't want to get stuck!' I added.

We made our way through the smelly tunnel full of damp, newly dug earth and when we

found a litter of baby badgers we could both
sense their panic.

I realised at once that they were blind. I had
to explain what the danger was and hope
that they would trust me enough to follow.
Clearly they were petrified. I sent Chickpea
back to the Athelstan tree. We needed an
interpreter. A few minutes later she came
back with Yulia riding on her back, holding
tightly to her collar.

Yulia explained in a softly pitched soothing
voice exactly what we needed the baby
badgers to do. The black and white striped
grey bundle started squirming and one

173

by one they stood up. I led them out into daylight and across the woodland floor, with Chickpea and Yulia bringing up the rear. We counted six cubs and shepherded them into the Athelstan tree.

'I'll look after them until the danger passes,' said Yulia.

'CHICK-PEA! RO-LO!...RO-LO!' Agitated voices and shrill whistles were just the other side of the bushes and we had to go quickly to avoid our owners finding the Athelstan tree. We knew the baby badgers would be safe with Yulia.

We were both firmly told off for ignoring our owners and attached to our leads. I winked at Chickpea. We didn't care; we had saved the badger cubs.

As we walked past the car park, I noticed a council van with some men in boiler suits stowing some sort of equipment back in the van. Their mission had been foiled by two smart Jack Russells. The badgers could shelter in the Athelstan tree until they could make themselves new homes, once the danger had passed.

Athelstan told me he was very pleased with my assistance in the badger saving operation and that my reward would be to travel anywhere I wanted to go in the time tunnel.

I thought about this for a moment and then remembered holiday photographs I had seen in the smiley lady's house of the pyramids of Ancient Egypt. That's where I wanted to go! I dreamt of pyramids and the Sphinx!

'Come back tonight!' said Athelstan 'and we'll see where the tunnel takes you.'

I could hardly wait for the house to fall silent so I could set off on my special adventure. The time tunnel would have to send me far back in history and a very long way indeed from the familiarity of England. Through the trapdoor, down the garden steps, under

The Secret Adventures of Rolo

the rickety gate and through the forest to the Athelstan tree. I dropped the pink ball and entered the Understory. Yulia was waiting.

The tunnel brought me out into a very hot and sandy place. As soon as I crawled out, the overwhelming heat hit me; that and the smell of camels and the sight of swaying palm trees.

I could hear chip-chip-chipping just in front of me and I spied a sculptor hard at work with a large chisel surrounded by a team of helpers creating a monument in limestone and it looked to me as if it was to have the body and legs of a lion. With imagination it could even have been a big dog.

I cast my eye to the great triangular shaped slabs behind me. They looked like giant pieces of chocolate. My curiosity got the better of me and I trotted over the hot sand as fast as I could for it was burning my paws, until I stood at the tiny entrance to the smallest of the pyramids.

Once inside, it was cool, musty and dark
and being an experienced tunneller I was
quite used to that. I followed a succession of
ladders and passageways and found myself
inside the base in what appeared to be a large
storage room.

I looked about, acclimatising my eyes to
the darkness from the contrast of the bright
desert sun and then realised oil lamps were
lighting the scene before me.

I knew at once what was going on because
I'd seen it in the floppy haired boy's school
books: mummification!

The soon-to-be inhabitant of this huge

monument was laid out on a slab and several physicians were in the process of embalming him. I sidled round a whole palaceful of furniture and precious possessions and ducked under what looked like a chariot wheel. I was startled when I heard a voice. It was a cat. No ordinary moggie but a sleek Egyptian feline and my instincts to give chase were quashed as I remembered that I was time travelling and had to put my natural desires to one side.

'I've not seen one like you before!' she purred. 'Are you a descendant of Anubis?'

Now, my ancient history is a little limited but I do know that Anubis was the Egyptian god with the head of a jackal, and he always oversaw matters of the dead. By the looks of the poor chap on the slab he was definitely dead!

'Yes, he's sent me in his place to learn,' I murmured, adding rather feebly 'I'm new.'

'Well, hello New, I'm Habibah,' the cat replied, her green eyes glinting in the darkness of the tomb. I thought it too complicated to explain, so I let it go.

'Why are all these worldly goods collected here? ' I asked, surveying the ornate chairs, tables, gold crockery, clothes and jewellery being laid out by servants in rows with mathematical precision, filling the whole floor space. The base of the pyramid resembled some kind of grand garage sale.

'To accompany the pharaoh to the afterlife of course! Goodness New, you certainly are wet behind the ears!'Habibah exclaimed.

She stood tall, with her four paws gathered in and her noble head erect.

'What are you doing here then?' I asked.

'I was his favourite companion, my name means 'loved' and I am to accompany him on his next journey,' she said rather proudly.

'What, you mean stay here forever in this tomb?' I asked, astonished.

'We will go on to the afterlife together,' she replied quietly. 'He wouldn't leave me behind; I am his cat for life.'

I saw four big stone jars neatly lined up under the slab. I asked Habibah what they were for and then wished I hadn't!

She told me each canopic jar contained the stomach, liver, lungs and intestines of the pharaoh and each organ was stored separately with a different god looking after them.

Enjoying my discomfort, she added that the pharaoh's brains had been poked around with a hook up his nose and then his body turned onto its side so that the mushed brains could be poured into a bowl for separate storage. Eeeeeuuuuwwwww! Way too much information I thought.

Habibah assured me that the heart was still inside the pharaoh's body as he would need that for his journey. Thank goodness I hadn't arrived forty days earlier or I would have witnessed this gruesome first stage of the mummification process!

I didn't even have to see the gaping cavities where the organs had been removed from, as these wounds had already been stuffed with resin soaked strips of linen – thank goodness for that!

Habibah explained that the body had lain these past weeks covered in salt and this was now the 'washing off' stage and then oil and finally resin would be applied to preserve the body. She told me with great delight that the corpse at this stage in the mummification process was darker and thinner than it had been at the time of death.

Luckily I only got to see the good bit – the wrapping with linen strips and I watched as amulets (kinds of charms) were hidden

The Secret Adventures of Rolo

in the bandages to ensure good luck and protection in the afterlife.

Another man of some importance entered the room; the royal make-up artist with his pots and paints, and then he produced a splendid wig which was carefully arranged around the royal head.

The mummy was then lifted by four solemn servants of a higher order than the furniture stackers, and laid in an ornate inner casket ready for the fitting of the elaborate funerary mask.

I knew all about that already because I'd seen a photograph of the blue and gold mask of Tutankhamun, now in the Cairo Museum; a postcard was on the smiley lady's fridge.

I wondered what all this high ceremony was for and asked my learned cat friend (I use the term loosely).

Habibah explained, in hushed tones, that

the body and the soul had to be separated and that the soul would then journey to the underworld where Osiris would judge it. If the pharaoh was deemed to have been a good person in his earthly life, then his soul and body would be reunited in the afterlife to live on through eternity. It was important for the soul to recognise the body when they met again and so the embalmer's job was to make the body in death look much as it had in life. That job required great skill indeed.

The outer casket was richly decorated with pure gold leaf and I noticed it was covered with hieroglyphics explaining to whom the body belonged in symbols and pictures. The lid was finally closed. The white robed men withdrew and I saw a shadow lengthening as the stone door of the tomb was about to be sealed up from the outside world forever.

'Are you sure you're staying here?' I asked Habibah.

'Perfectly sure,' she replied, settling into her

statuesque pose and closing her green eyes.

'Right then, I'll be off – very nice to have made your acquaintance,' I said with as much dignity as I could muster. It was all I could do not to break into a run in my effort to cross the floor as quickly as possible; such was my fear of being locked in.

I remembered the trauma of being locked in a cage during my last spell in the dogs home. (That's why have a black smudge above my nose.)

I made it to the door, with a few inches of daylight remaining, and poked my nose around it. A sandalled foot pushed me with some force back inside the pyramid.

'The pharaoh's animals stay with him; all of them,' I heard a gruff voice say, and then all sound was muffled by the rolling of the stone and the sealing of the tomb.

I tried to protest, scrabbling at the closed up

entrance, but the serene cat was by my side again.

'It's no good. Look, my family all have to stay here too. I wish it could be otherwise for them. It is my destiny, not theirs.'

I looked where she was pointing and saw several kittens huddled together in the dwindling lamp light.

'There must be another way out!' I exclaimed. I was sure that Athelstan hadn't sent me all the way to Egypt to spend my last few days entombed with a bunch of cats!

Inspecting the walls for another means of exit, I saw a statue of Anubis standing on a plinth. I pretended to the young cats that it

The Secret Adventures of Rolo

was me.

'You don't look much like Anubis…your nose isn't long enough' said one of the kittens called Masud.

His mother reprimanded him for being cheeky.

On closer scrutiny I saw a tiny trapdoor in the plinth underneath the foot of the long-nosed, standing-up black dog statue. Large enough for me at any rate.

'Anyone want to come with me?' I asked casually, sensing an escape route and not wanting to hang around much longer.

Masud scampered away from his brothers and sisters and, with a look back at his mother, said 'I do.' The others swiftly followed, like sheep.

Without waiting for anyone to try to stop us, I pushed the trapdoor open just enough to exit through and held it open. Masud squeezed through first, followed by Mandisa, Manu, Mensah and Mert. All looked pretty much the same to me; small grey cats with sleek fur and all with their mother's glittering green eyes.

187

'Live up to your name,' the mother cat called after her eldest and cheekiest son as the last tail retreated and 'look after him Akins' she addressed to me. It seemed she'd given me a new name.

When we emerged in the full hot sun of the Egyptian desert I asked him what the name 'Masud' meant.

'Lucky,' he replied, and Manu 'born second' and Mensah 'born third' and my sister Mandisa means 'sweet'.

'What about Mert?' I asked, looking at the quietest and smallest kitten.

'Oh I forgot him; the 'silent one' replied Masud.

'You're not from round here are you? Oh, and if you're wondering, mother called you Akins which means 'Brave Boy', he added.

Wow! I'd never been called that before. It had a certain ring to it. I liked it.

The Secret Adventures of Rolo

Night was falling fast and at last the sand was cooling down, as was the air temperature. Better to travel in the total darkness, I thought. Less chance of detection by the guards who seemed determined to see all animals entombed.

We were a strange party, and dog and kittens stopped in the shadow of the giant half-finished sculpture to rest, waiting for the cover of night to creep over the desert. The sculptor and his team of helpers had already gone home.

'What do you think it's going to be?' I asked Masud, nodding in the direction of the statue.

He had no idea but then I saw a mischievous glint in his eye and he climbed up onto the plinth and used the scaffolding to pull himself up the height of the half-finished beast to the spot where the face should be. It was still a sheer block of smooth limestone. He called his brothers and sister to join him.

189

The Secret Adventures of Rolo

Sensing adventure and fun, they didn't need asking twice.

'Stay where you are Akins!' he called, and he set to work at once with his paws. Four pairs of glittering green eyes watched in amazement and then more paws and claws joined in.

I must confess I dozed off, and awoke stiffly in the dawn, stretching forwards and backwards doing my usual yoga routine. It took me a while to realise where I was.

'Now do you recognise it, Akins?' shouted Masud from the top of the scaffolding.

The Secret Adventures of Rolo

Rubbing my eyes with my front paws in the rosy coloured sunlight of dawn, I glanced up at the sculpture and burst out laughing. Masud and his siblings had copied the exact features of my head on to the lion's body! It was a very good likeness indeed and I felt immensely proud to be part of Egypt's rich ancient history. A worthy monument at last!

'We'd better get going' I said, after I'd admired their handiwork from all angles. I didn't want to tear myself away and wished I'd had something to capture the image to show Athelstan and the woodland folk but was conscious of the time.

I would love to have seen the sculptor's face when he realised someone had finished his monument for him! Wonder if he'd have to change it back to whatever it was supposed to be.

I found the time tunnel entrance easily enough, but the kittens couldn't cross the threshold.

The Secret Adventures of Rolo

'Can't we bring them to Athelstan?' I asked Yulia when she appeared with her lantern, already suspecting what the answer might be.

'No, I'm afraid these kittens won't be able to time travel; you'll have to leave them here in their own time,' Yulia replied, confirming my fear. I turned to Masud and told him with sadness that they would have to stay in Ancient Egypt.

'Don't worry, Akins; you rescued my family, and thanks to you and your discovery of the trapdoor I can go back in there and persuade mother to come out and we can all find new owners…don't worry about us… it's been nice knowing you, Salaam Alekum,' he waved goodbye, adding, 'We'll remember you because we will always see your face in the desert!' as he waved a proud paw at his artwork.

Such an artistic talent was wasted on small

cats. Impressive though. Handsome chap, the model, and a rather good likeness I thought, though I say so myself.

Dog Blog #5 — According to Rolo

I have had a bit of trouble catching up on my forty winks these last few mornings. There's a family of magpies out there hopping about from roof to roof shrieking and cackling away, calling and answering. If you're on at them now Mrs, just wait until they're teenagers, I thought to myself.

I know magpies are in the crow family and that they are attracted to bright objects and will steal them for their nest. They have even been known to steal clothes pegs! When humans see one of these black and white birds on its own they think it's the bringer of sorrow so

they will always look for another…
or even shout, 'How are you today,
where's your wife, your child and
your family?' because the more of
them you see the luckier it is.

That led me to think about the
other birds in the crow family
that are often easily confused
because they are all black. Well,
I've been doing a bit of research
and can tell you that the jackdaw
has silvery white beady eyes and
greyish feathers on its neck and
back. The rook has grey skin at the
base of its beak and a flat forehead
which makes its head look pointed
overall. The crow has brown eyes
and neat feathers round the base
of its powerful black beak. So
there you are, now you can easily
identify the different black birds
in the crow family!

Chapter 13

Rolo Recognised

I was still a bit tired a few days later. I woke with a start as I heard a tap-tap-tapping of a bird beak on the window.

I thought it was the owl come to summon me and then realised it was a wren gathering nesting material from the conservatory gutter. I snuggled down in my basket and went back to sleep, pleased to have a bit of a lie-in. Time travel can be exhausting you know.

We were off to see Grandad Polo today. The smiley lady goes to visit him every week and I usually accompany her. I don't mind because it's a long way and I can sleep in the car. The other residents of the care home love me because I know how to behave when I am around the older generation. Today was an unusual day, however, because the floppy haired boy was with us. He doesn't like long car journeys and often feels travel sick.

To take his mind off his queasiness and to stop his moaning, the smiley lady explained the rules of 'Pub Cricket'. This is something she used to play with her parents to while away a long car journey. It doesn't really work on motorways, though, only if you are driving through towns.

I took it all in, and will do my best to explain the rules to you in case you want to play it sometime.

The first player is nominated to 'bat' and all occupants of the car have to keep their eyes peeled for a pub sign.

If the picture on the sign has any legs on

it, these are added to the players score. For example, The Dog and Duck would score 6 as the picture has 6 legs. The Fox and Hounds would score maximum 20 points as there are probably too many legs to count. If you see a pub without any legs on its sign for example, The Duke's Head or the Somerset Arms you are 'out' and play passes on to the next player. You keep a running score and can continue the game over several car journeys. By the way, if you see a pub called The Eighth Army you would automatically win the game!

Our journey started with the floppy haired boy 'batting' first and he was delighted to start with The Red Lion which gave him four legs. Next was The Duke of York (all of him, not just his head!) so that gave him another two runs. The next pub sign we passed was 'The Red House' and so he was out and the play passed to the smiley lady whilst the floppy haired boy retained a total of six runs. The smiley lady was out for a duck (zero runs) as the next pub sign showed 'The Queen's Head' definitely not any legs. It didn't seem that I was playing, so I nodded off for the rest of the journey, lulled by the smooth gear changes and the warmth of the March sun through the car window. I opened an eye when the floppy haired boy shouted out that he'd seen 'The Dog and Bone' and he refused to accept that it would only score four points because he reasoned it was possibly a leg bone and therefore worth five points. The smiley lady gave in with good grace and concentrated on the traffic.

When we got to Grandad Polo's home, he was sat in his wheelchair out in the garden, taking in the mild spring air. He was very pleased to see us.

As usual I was fussed over by carers and residents alike. Everyone loves me, and I am given little bits of biscuit and cake when the smiley lady isn't looking.

I love visiting Grandad Polo and I also get

to hoover him for crumbs after he's eaten a homemade rock cake that the smiley lady has made and brought him in a tin. We both especially love them when they're still slightly warm from the oven, Grandad Polo and I.

The sun shone brightly in the March sky and the smiley lady remarked to Grandad Polo that it was still a bit chilly out as she wrapped a fleece around his shoulders. She wheeled him around the garden to look at the new growth of the primroses and daffodils poking their bright yellow heads up over the brickwork of the raised bed, built for ease of maintenance by people who could no longer stand up due to age or infirmity.

The smiley lady took Grandad Polo indoors to see the hatching chicks which were going to be reared in the care home and live in the garden and called us in to have a look. The floppy haired boy and I stared at the cracking eggs with tiny sharp beaks and yellow balls of fluff emerging from them. The smiley lady told the floppy haired boy to take me back outside and that she must remember to keep me on my lead when the chickens were released in the garden. I wonder why that was?

We sat down on a bench again and I hopped up next to the floppy haired boy. An elderly gentleman, whom I don't recall seeing before, shuffled over in his slippers, leaning heavily on his walking frame. He was being helped along by one of my favourite carers called Sarah who always made a big fuss of me and slipped me non-doggy treats, like digestive biscuits, when no one was looking.

200

'Have you met Rolo?' she asked the man in a kindly voice. The elderly gentleman peered at me through crinkly eyes and broke into a smile and said, 'I do believe we have met.'

Sarah told the floppy haired boy in a stage whisper that she thought this was highly unlikely as Mr Jenkins had only recently moved into the residential care home, but she nodded and agreed politely and pulled up a chair behind him.

Mr Jenkins sat down heavily, easing himself to be more comfortable within reach of me and I sat patiently whilst he fondled my ears with his big brown flecked hands and stroked me firmly all the while leaning on his frame.

He smelt of Imperial Leather soap and peppermints. I watched him reach into his top pocket for a handkerchief and he mopped his brow, letting out a sigh. Sarah the carer, seeing him safely settled in a chair, patted him on the shoulder and went off

The Secret Adventures of Rolo

to attend to someone else who was calling for her help and the floppy haired boy and elderly gentleman sat in companionable silence as the young and the aged often do.

I sat quietly with my paws gathered in, looking down at my feet as I thought it might be impolite to stare.

'I have met you before you know,' whispered Mr Jenkins in a slightly raspy voice, 'a very long time ago, in London, when I was a boy and you came to my rescue.'

The floppy haired boy nodded politely and probably thought Mr Jenkins' mind was playing tricks on him, as so often happened with Grandad Polo these days, but the elderly gentleman was quite positive in his identification. Tears welled up in his cloudy eyes and he bent down and hugged me close and I saw at close range and I was engulfed in a cloud of Imperial Leather soap and peppermints once more. I licked his hand to show that I cared.

Sarah appeared and took his arm, 'Come on then, Nick, let's get you back indoors,' as she eased him out of his chair.

'How about a nice cup of tea and a biscuit? I think we've got your favourites.' The floppy haired boy looked around the garden wondering where his mum and Grandad Polo had got to.

I remembered exactly who Nick was and indeed when we had first met.

I slept all the way home, and I don't know if the smiley lady and floppy haired boy resumed their game of Pub Cricket or not.

Dog Blog #6 According to Rolo

The next morning I woke early and was let out into the garden for my early morning patrol to make sure everything was as it should be. I stand at the top of the garden steps and slowly move my head from

203

right to left, surveying my patch.

I trotted back inside and waited
patiently in meerkat position for
my biscuit. Suddenly I heard a loud
shriek from the smiley lady and I
ran at once towards the lounge.
She shut the door firmly with me
on the outside so I pressed my
nose to the window as if we were
playing Hide the Biscuit, and tried
to see through the frosted glass,
wondering what on earth had caused
her alarm.

She shouted upstairs to the floppy
haired boy, who was late for school
again,
'Shut Rolo outside the lounge; come
quickly, I need your help!'

He came downstairs with wet hair
and nothing but a towel around his

waist.

'What's up, Mum?'

He went into the lounge and kept me behind the door. I tried to rush through his legs and round the door but he closed it with me still on the outside. Peering through the frosted glass I could see a small black shadow fluttering about in the lounge. From what the smiley lady was saying to the floppy haired boy, evidently the shape had plopped down the chimney.

The Secret Adventures of Rolo

The black shape had settled on the coffee table and was not moving much, only breathing with its beak slightly open. It looked a bit stunned.

'Don't take your eyes off it,' said the smiley lady as she moved slowly around the lounge, opening windows in the hope that the startled young fledgling would take itself off outside.

There was a bit of a stand-off going on in the lounge.

The bird sat there blinking and didn't seem in a hurry to exit. The smiley lady was worried it would get in a flap and start flying around the room again.

'I've got to go — sorry Mum,' said

the floppy haired boy and he opened
the lounge door which I was pressed
up against, watching proceedings.
I fell into the lounge and of
course the bird in panic rose and
flew straight out through the open
window.

I didn't really know what all the
fuss was about. Why didn't they
involve me in the first place?

Dog Blog #7 According to Rolo

Me again. Just had the opportunity
to get on the laptop whilst they're
upstairs.

I hadn't seen Chickpea for a while
and was pleased to bump into her on
a walk one evening in June. Summer
had snuck up almost unexpectedly.
Longer lighter evenings were upon

us and the promise of fine weather.

Of course longer days meant short adventuring time for me in the night time but I didn't mind. Sunny days meant happy walks with the smiley lady and new territories to explore.

Chickpea and I greeted each other in the usual way and I noticed a crowd of neighbours standing in the field looking up at a tall ash tree and pointing. Merlin and Jasper and their owners were there too. When I cocked an ear up I could hear the most incredible sound. The notes were piercing and tuneful and each trill was repeated twice before the tune changed. Searching for the source of the song, the humans were passing around a pair of binoculars and someone said it was a nightingale.

'There he is!' someone shouted and pointed to the branch at the top of the tree.

The songster turned out to be a very ordinary looking little brown bird, but boy oh boy could he sing! Once heard never forgotten.

Next time I saw Da I asked him about the nightingale and he said: 'The nightingale can usually first be heard some time in May or June.

They are short stay visitors and will depart again for warmer climes anytime between July and September depending on the weather. They are famously noted for their singing voices which few can match for dexterity with high and low notes in quick succession. You are very lucky to have heard one.'

It was about this time I noticed something odd about the wheat fields. They hadn't been planted with cereals this year as was usual; in fact the farmer planted them rather late and the neighbours were all discussing the strange crop, and analysing the new growth, saying it looked like poppies. Merlin's dad said it might be to commemorate the centenary of the outbreak of the First World War but Jasper's mum said it was more

The Secret Adventures of Rolo

likely to be a source of medical morphine. Over the next few weeks we watched the young plants grow taller and flower white with pink middles. Then when the petals fell off, the seed pods looked like Aliens and they swelled up with the rain. We watched, waiting for them to be harvested.

I made an amusing observation whilst walking along the banks of the River Kennet at Manton. The smiley lady pointed out a group of Canada geese bobbing about on the calm water near the bridge by the church.

211

'Do you know that a group of geese on the ground are called a 'gaggle' and a group of geese in flight are called a 'skein',' she said to a passer-by who was peering into the shallow water looking to see a brown trout.

'I wonder what you call geese on the water then,' the man pondered.

Neither knew the answer to that. They stood for a while exchanging favourite collective nouns.

'A parliament of owls!' said the smiley lady.

'A quarrel of sparrows!' the man retaliated.

'An embarrassment of red-faced warblers!' the smiley lady rose admirably to the challenge.

'A co-operation of coots!' the man warmed to the theme. I am not sure which were real and which were made up.

'An ostentation of peacocks!' the smiley lady played her trump card.

I think perhaps they both like their crossword puzzles.

'A flotilla of geese?' I said helpfully, but of course neither heard me. Sometimes it's frustrating being a small dog.

The smiley lady had the last word;

'A rascal of Jack Russells?' and she hooted with laughter.

The Secret Adventures of Rolo

Dog blog #8 - According to Rolo

So the nightingale has gone quiet; maybe its babies have left the nest and it doesn't feel the need to show off anymore. It's a shame because I was being taken for an extra evening walk just to hear him!

This evening the jolly lady came over and we walked down to the Outside Chance for a fundraising pub quiz. The jolly lady and the smiley lady wanted to be a team of two, not counting me. They didn't ask me for any answers to the quiz but they did call themselves eight legs and a waggy tail. I must say they were pretty useless at dingbats and geography when the map of Africa got passed around, although they surprised me on the

sports round and as expected, they are experts of food and drink.
I sat quietly under the table observing things. I knew quite a few answers because I watch a lot of Pointless on television. Heigh ho…another blue sky day. Out for more walkies soon I hope…

The Secret Adventures of Rolo

Chapter 14

Rolo meets Shakespeare

The floppy haired boy was doing his homework.

'Mum, why didn't Shakespeare write about dogs in his plays?' he asked, chewing his pencil. I was pretending to be asleep, curled at his feet under the dining room table, but I raised an ear all the better to listen.

'I think there are a couple of them mentioned in 'The Two Gentlemen of Verona,' said the smiley lady, stirring the custard in the kitchen.

'I had a friend who had to lend her greyhounds to a Stratford production one year,' she continued.

The floppy haired boy went back to his homework. I thought about this.

'Look, Mum, Rolo's doing clown eyes again!'

The Secret Adventures of Rolo

I had a vision of a chimney pop into my head.

When I next saw Athelstan in the forest I told him I'd like to go and meet William Shakespeare.

'And why would you want to do that I wonder?' he smiled. 'But be warned, he doesn't like dogs.'

Via the usual means of time travel, I found myself in the middle of 17th century Stratford-upon-Avon. I immediately saw a greyhound who reminded me of de Grys who I'd once met on Marlborough Common during a time travelling adventure last year.

'Excuse me,' I said politely once we'd sniffed each other in greeting. 'Could you please show me the way to the writer William Shakespeare's house?'

'I should steer well clear if I were you. He doesn't care for dogs,' the Greyhound replied.

I was beginning to feel a sense of foreboding, but I followed his directions, which took me along a winding cart track into a hamlet.

I sneaked into a low ceilinged thatched cottage and knew immediately I was in the right place. The chimney was smoking terribly filling the cluttered cottage with the smell of wood smoke.

A balding man sat at the wooden kitchen table scratching away with a feather pen, making black spiders on the blank page.

I hid under a sideboard and watched him fill sheet after sheet with spidery writing, pausing only occasionally to dip his quill in the fresh ink stored in a bottle in front of him.

He was muttering to himself and his body racked with coughs. I wasn't really surprised; the smoke in the room was quite thick and was pouring out of the fireplace. The writer didn't seem to notice.

Suddenly the coughing man caught sight of me and threw his feather pen down with a curse and made a splot on the paper.

'Now look what you've made me do! Get out dog!'

I kept close to the floor and sidled towards the door. He resumed his writing and mumbling and I could hear,

"Friends, Romans, countrymen, lend me your ears."

'Excuse me, sir,' I piped up. 'That doesn't make sense.'

The great poet and playwright put down his quill carefully, placed both hands on the table and leant towards me,

'How dare you criticise me? Don't you know who I am?' he thundered and then added less thunderously, 'What on earth do you mean 'it doesn't make sense'?

He broke off in a fit of coughing.

Emboldened now that I had the great man's attention I said

'You really should get that chimney seen to. There must be a blockage. Now, where was I? How can someone lend you their ears? You can't detach your ears. Sorry it just doesn't work for me.'

'It's a figure of speech!' he roared, waving his quill at me.

'I suppose you don't like 'But, soft! What light through yonder window breaks?' either?'

'Well I don't really understand it if I'm honest…why don't you just say 'the sun is shining'?'

'I'M NOT WRITING FOR DOGS!' He roared suddenly pushing back his chair and it fell with a clatter onto the flagstone floor.

The Secret Adventures of Rolo

Shakespeare was seized with another bout of smoke-induced coughing.

I took a deep breath (it was smoke free near the floor) and said, as calmly as I could,

'It's just that your language is a bit flowery. School children have to study your plays and learn chunks of speech off by heart… the floppy haired boy struggles…they all do.' I could sense that I was only inflaming the situation. I decided to try a different tack,

'Look,' I said trying to dig myself out of the hole. 'I can help you clear the blockage in the chimney but you'll have to put the fire out and we must wait for the flue to cool down. That could take some time.'

Shakespeare stood up and poured himself a drink from a pitcher into a pewter tankard and cut a hunk of bread and a wedge of cheese. He pushed some towards me, pouring water in a bowl and setting it at the other end of the table.

'There,' he instructed, inviting me to sit up at the table on a stool.

'Now look here, I don't care much for dogs. I wrote a small part for a couple of greyhounds in 'The Two Gentlemen of Verona' recently but I didn't give them a significant part; I didn't think they were up to it. I'm a cat man myself. Have you seen these two? They sleep under my four poster bed.'

I glanced over at the deep window ledge and saw a black cat he introduced as Othello and an angry hissing cat called Macbeth. The tone of his voice had changed when he talked about his cats.

Because I was time travelling I knew I would have to be polite to them or if at all possible, just ignore them.

In reality I wanted to chase the stupid smirks off their big smug furry faces. Both cats eyed me mistrustfully. I doubted they had any idea that they would inspire central characters in their master's later plays!

'So, dog, how do you propose we spend the time waiting for the chimney to cool?'

'Maybe I could help you write a play?' I looked up coyly, seizing the main chance, and did 'clown eyes' at him. (Well, it worked with the smiley lady and the floppy haired boy.)

To my surprise Shakespeare started laughing. His shoulders were heaving as he laughed so much that tears ran down his face and into his beard.

He staggered to the fireplace when he had enough control of himself and upended a pitcher of water onto the hearth, dousing the flames.

I followed him out into the courtyard, where he worked the handle of the water pump and filled another pitcher and that too ended up in the fireplace.

The hearth sizzled and the smoke in the room increased for a moment. Even the cats vacated the window ledge and went outside.

When the smoke had cleared we re-entered the room and Shakespeare pushed the food platters aside and righted the ink pot on the table, taking a fresh piece of vellum to write upon.

'I've decided to humour you, sirrah; what will be the subject of your play?'

Hmm, I hadn't thought this far ahead. I put my head in my paws and thought for a moment. I tried to remember the plays that the floppy haired boy had talked about over the tea table when struggling with his English homework.

'How about 'The Merry Dogs of Marlborough'?' I said. The bearded face broke into a broad grin. He obviously liked this idea.

'And what's the plot going to be?'

'Well, I thought you could write about one of your best loved characters, that fat old man Falstaff, the one you wrote about in the history plays.' I hoped the great man was impressed with my knowledge of his works.

'Whoah! Let me stop you right there smartypaws. Falstaff died in one of my history plays, Henry V I think it was!' Shakespeare banged his fist on the table and then added, 'Actually I'm rather sorry I did write him out because he was a very popular character with the groundlings at The Globe. I keep getting booed since I killed him off.'

'Then why don't you bring him back?' I suggested.

'Don't be so silly!' he sneered. 'I can't bring him back from the dead! So what other great ideas do you have for this play, young dog?'

'Well, I haven't thought it out exactly, but I

225

thought we'd set the scene in a lovely English garden, and have some woodland folk in it (I have a couple of characters in mind), and maybe one of the human characters gets turned into a donkey? I'll play the lead and then there's my girlfriend Chickpea. We could get the theme of mixed-up-love in it of course – always a crowd pleaser.' I was warming to my theme.

226

The Secret Adventures of Rolo

'And I suppose you want me to call this farce 'Rolo and Chickpea'?' he bellowed.

Shakespeare might have been snorting outwardly at my suggestions, but I could see him scratching away on the sheet of paper in front of him. The quill never stopped moving. He was going along with the idea of 'The Merry Dogs of Marlborough' and in spite of all his sneering I was sure he secretly liked the plot.

I kept my end of the bargain. As soon as the chimney had cooled enough I clambered up it, finding paw holes in the warm stone work.

I think a dog had been up that chimney before; I doubt it had been one of those useless cats.

The cats sat washing on the windowsill. They eyed me with disdain; I think the expression is 'like something the cat brought in.'

I bumped into something spiky in the flue

and realised I'd found the cause of the smoke in the room. There was a rather large and empty bird's nest blocking the chimney. I head butted it a few times and moved to one side to let the sticks, mud and straw fall into the sodden hearth below.

I climbed a bit higher and knew the chimney was now clear. Satisfied my work was complete and that the fire would now draw properly, I scampered back down the chimney and landed in the hearth in a cloud of black dust and twigs.

'Stay where you are!' the playwright boomed as I sat blinking in a pool of soot which had blackened the rushes covering the floor. Without further ado he picked me up by the scruff of my neck and marched me out at arm's length to the water pump, working the handle furiously to get the flow going and dousing me thoroughly to get rid of the soot, without any care to my wellbeing or comfort.

'Thou art as dark as night,' he muttered and I thought that was actually quite good and said so. That earned me another dunking under the freezing water spout. He rubbed me dry with a towel. (Much more roughly than the smiley lady ever does, I might add.) I put up with it. I could sense that the cats were still smirking on the windowsill.

Shakespeare then reached for a taper, and lighting it in a tallow candle he re-lit the fire and his face broke into a smile when the wood burned cleanly, and this time the smoke went up the chimney without any problem. He invited me to sit beside it on the cleaned rushes to dry off.

After a few moments, I shook myself dry and then glanced over at the beginning of the collaborative play on the table.

I was very pleased with what I saw. A whole ream of paper. I asked the bard if he would put my name on it as co-author.

'Zounds!' I was silenced by the ink pot whizzing past my ear and smashing behind me in the fireplace, splattering me with black dots.

The Secret Adventures of Rolo

'Thou art a cheeky fellow! This is MY play – I don't write WITH anyone!'

'I'll take that as a no then,' I said, as I skittered towards the door. 'You'll be hearing from my lawyer!'

'Thou art a spotty dog,' he spluttered and I thought to myself, that's quite good! I wonder if I'll get written into one of his plays.

As I trotted down the garden path I heard the unmistakable sound of the screwing up of paper and the ensuing crackle as the whole manuscript was consigned to the nicely burning fire. Black smoke from the chimney bore testimony to the fact that The Merry Dogs of Marlborough had just gone up in flames.

I have to confess I was rather disappointed as I thought I had some really good ideas there. At least I had my answer as to why there were no dogs in Shakespeare's plays!

I nodded at Athelstan who was smiling at me from his bark perch. I scampered home and squeezed under the rickety gate and up the garden steps and back through the trapdoor under the sink.

When I got back into my basket in the kitchen I failed to notice anything was amiss and fell into a deep sleep, dreaming of curtain calls and taking a bow on stage in the theatre. I would have to work on my bow.

It wasn't until the next afternoon, rolling on the floor with the floppy haired boy, that he noticed:

'Mum, come look, Rolo's grown another black spot on his back!'

Dog Blog #9 — According to Rolo

Seizing the moment to update you whilst they are at the shops.

The Secret Adventures of Rolo

I had a wonderful day out on Sunday. I was a bit worried at first because I was bundled into the car and the next thing I knew we were back at Dogs Trust near Newbury — I thought the smiley lady had brought me here to choose another rescue dog, or, even worse, to replace me!

I needn't have worried though; it was their annual dog show and I have never seen so many dogs of all shapes and sizes and breeds in one place. It really was a glorified puppy club! Thought I even recognised a couple of my old pals from a couple of years ago.

The smiley lady set out a table with the fake Rolo soft toy perched on top of a pile of my books. I just had to sit under the table in the shade — it was a very hot day —

and look proud.

Lots of children and adults, too,
came by to stroke me and talk to
me. I am a famous dog. As you know,
I love attention!

The smiley lady was happy because
she sold lots of books. We gave a
donation to Dogs Trust, of course.
I even took part in the dog show…I
had to sit in the ring for the
Handsomest Dog category (can't
believe I didn't win) but if they'd
had a category for the smartest dog
who writes books, time travels,
shares nature notes and blogs, well
I would have won it paws down!

The smiley lady didn't enter me for
'the dog the judge would most like
to take home' as she didn't want to
draw too much attention to the fact

I am a very gifted dog, and she wouldn't part with me anyway.

When I got a bit hot and started panting, I was cooled down with wet towels and paddled in a doggy paddling pool with all the other dogs. Nobody fought or even growled — it was a very sociable event and I loved it. The smiley lady said it was so nice to see people out with their dogs as there truly aren't many places where we are welcomed. I have a sneaky suspicion we might be doing a whole round of dog shows in future!

It's very hot — not that I'm complaining — so I spend a lot of time indoors and then I go outside and stretch right out in the sun on the patio. Occasionally I get taken out for dip in the River Kennet.

It's a dog's life! Right, they're coming...must go...oh and I've had a strange dream about running rats!

Chapter 15

Rolo and the Black Death

Athelstan sent for me and told me my next task might well need the help of Chickpea. I didn't mind. Although she could be a bit annoying with her continual questioning, I have to admit I quite liked the company.

This time we were bound for 14th century Bristol at the height of the Black Death.

I'd overheard the floppy haired boy talking to his mum about recent theories about the plague being viral, and not spread by flea bites borne on the back of rats as previously thought, but the research had not proved conclusive and so the medieval rat was still in the frame as far as he was concerned.

I said to Chickpea full of confidence,

'Simple, we get rid of the rats and the fleas will disappear and the plague will die out, you mark my words.'

'I heard my family reading a bed time story once about the Pied Piper of Hamelin. It seems he was a musician who dressed in multi-coloured clothes and once used music to lure rats away from the town,' she replied.

'Hmmmm….let me think about this for a minute' I said.

'I can borrow a recorder but I don't know how to play it' chipped in Chickpea, trying to be helpful.

Recorder. Now that had given me an idea. All I had to do was find a piece of music that might drive rats to plunge into the sea – I already had the means of recording the music and playing it back.

'What sort of music do you think might send rats crazy and make them plummet to their deaths?' I asked Chickpea.

'Scraping violins…heavy metal…rap…screechy opera…bagpipes?' she said, hopefully.

'That's it!! We need to get hold of a recording of bagpipes; that should do the trick!'

I was very excited about the idea and knew exactly where to find one.

When the smiley lady and floppy haired boy went up to Scotland they came back with a CD of the music, but it was so mournful they couldn't listen to it. It was in the box room with the other junk.

Having managed to record the most wailing and miserable track featuring the drone of the pipes that I could find, I had to trust my judgement as I couldn't even check it for quality of recording because it was too painful to play it back.

I asked Athelstan if he'd like to listen as we prepared for our night time adventure, but he shook his head.

Yulia said, 'Make sure you keep that machine

well and truly turned off when we're in the time tunnel or it will send us all mad, and here, take this for your ears!'

She stuck a soft lump of something on the back of the tape recorder which I had looped around my neck.

With an air of anticipation, Chickpea and I entered the hole in the tree right behind Yulia, once we'd dropped the pink balls at Athelstan's feet.

We popped out on the other side with some trepidation.

We were travelling back to a time of great pestilence and if we weren't careful we might catch the plague ourselves and bring it back to the 21st century!

I told Chickpea that I'd heard the floppy haired boy say that in some parts of London the plague pits, where the victims of the deadly disease had been buried in mass graves, were still not allowed to be built on to this day for fear of re-infecting the population.

Yulia tied small handkerchiefs round our muzzles and then burst out laughing as she thought we resembled cowboys!

'I don't see the point of the mask,' said Chickpea, her words muffled by the handkerchief.

'Well, why do you think so many people in Asia wore masks when SARS broke out a few years ago? The idea is to stop germs spreading through the air.'

I have no idea where that knowledge came from, but it sounded impressive and it silenced Chickpea. Sometimes I surprise myself!

What we did know about the Black Death was that it struck fast and killed its victims within three or four days. The plague seemed a mixture of bubonic and pneumonic and didn't discriminate between wealthy and poor, young and old. It struck villages as well as cities. One thing seemed clear: poor sanitation and overcrowding didn't help as the disease spread quickly and there was no escaping it.

In London, the River Thames was a flowing cesspool, used for disposing of human waste as well as a source of drinking water. Rats were everywhere. When the King raised concerns about the state of the streets of the capital in 1349, he was told that nothing could be done about that because all the street cleaners had perished in the plague.

In London alone it was estimated that between a third and half the population had been wiped out.

Yulia advised us to keep an eye on each other for any sign of swellings or marks appearing in the area where our little legs joined our bodies. Frankly we were terrified! So much to think about! There we were arriving in Bristol in the Spring of 1350 with little more than handkerchiefs over our mouths to keep us safe! All our hopes lay in an old tape recorder and a hunch about the effect of bagpipe music on rodents.

The moans of the afflicted were the first thing we heard. Pitiful and wailing. Chickpea thought I'd turned on the tape recorder by mistake. Then we noticed the smell; the filth of the streets and contaminated water lying everywhere, and added to that the aroma of running sores and decomposing bodies. In short, the stench of the plague.

'Now what?' said Chickpea, her eyes watering as she mumbled through her handkerchief.

I suggested that we ran to the docks as this was the place most rats seemed to originate from, coming off ships in their droves.

Without hanging around too much and

gagging from the stench we headed down to the quayside and sure enough the place was teeming with rats. Millions of them. They all seemed to be on a mission running this way and that, scavenging for food and no doubt flea-ridden.

'Quick, get the tape recorder going,' said Chickpea, once we'd located the soft stuff which Yulia had given us to gently stuff in our own ears. It turned out to be beeswax.

We perched on the quayside and I pressed the 'play' button on the tape recorder, turning up the volume dial as high as I possibly could. The sounds of wailing and droning filled the air. Luckily the beeswax filtered out most of it so we didn't have to endure listening to it ourselves.

Miraculously the noise seemed to have the desired effect on the rats. They started frantically running round in circles, bumping into each other in their frenzy to escape the terrible noise coming out from

The Secret Adventures of Rolo

the machine. A smart rat tried to seize the
tape recorder. I had to shield it and snap at
him to keep him away. Alright I admit it; not
all rats are as stupid as I first thought.

Or are they? The rat who tried to stop the
racket ran instead to the edge of the quay,
and, as if he were magnetic, all the rest of
them started to follow. One by one the rats
plunged into the Bristol Channel to their

The Secret Adventures of Rolo

watery deaths and were not seen again.

I turned off the tape recorder with a resounding click. Thank goodness that was over.

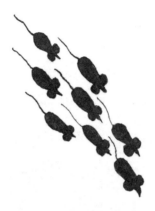

'Let's hope they took their fleas with them!' said Chickpea, anxious to remove her handkerchief from her mouth. She slipped it round her neck like a kerchief.

We couldn't wait to return to the time tunnel and we collapsed at Athelstan's feet. Yulia and Da made us roll in wet leaves at once; they were quite insistent. I wondered whether wet oak leaves really had antiseptic properties but didn't have the energy to start an argument.

Chickpea and I trotted off to our respective homes smelling of damp leaves and quite exhausted by our experience, minus the little hankies.

The smiley lady saw me scratch my neck the next morning. There was a little itchy bit just behind my right ear… I couldn't quite reach it with my back foot.

'Hmm, bath time Rolo, and I think it's time we renewed your anti- flea protection, I can't remember when we last did it, but I'm sure it must be due.'

Later that day, I was curled up with the floppy haired boy and he sneezed loudly. Twice. I shot off his lap. The smiley lady laughed.

'Rolo doesn't like it when people sneeze – he always moves away!'

247

Lady, if you'd seen what I'd seen in medieval Bristol you would avoid sneezers too.

I stretched out on the floor and thought about floating in space.

Chapter 16

Rolo in Space

'Rolo you're going to love this next adventure,' said Yulia as I stepped once more into the Athelstan tree and wondered where I was bound.

'This is unlike anything you've ever done before. You have to be a brave little dog and we can't wait to hear all about your adventure.'

'Where am I going?' I wondered.

'To the USSR; what you would know as Russia. Baikonur Cosmodrome, the first and largest space station in the world, to be precise.'

'Do you mean I'm going to travel in space?' I said in awe.

'Do you want to?' asked Yulia mischievously.

'Isn't it a bit dangerous?' I was fighting to

The Secret Adventures of Rolo

keep down my natural terrier shake.

'Don't worry, Paddy Paws. Athelstan has picked out a particular space mission for you, on board Sputnik 9. We know this one goes well.'

I couldn't help but think how jealous the other dogs would be. How cool was that? Rolo, Astrodog…no, wait, if it's a Russian space mission then I'll be a Cosmodog!

'Pyat….chye-tir-ye….tree…dva…a-deen…. vzletat!' The loud and steady countdown boomed over the tannoy. I braced myself and felt the G force wobbling my face as we took off at goodness knows how many miles per hour!

I looked around at my companions (or maybe I should say comrades). There was a guinea pig, absolutely cacking itself in the bottom of its cage, and a handful of white mice.

The Secret Adventures of Rolo

I am not too keen on rodents since the Black Death adventure, but, hey ho, they are my travel companions and I have to be polite.

I smiled and said 'dobroye utro' which I believe means 'good morning'. Their pink eyes stared at me blankly. Well, except for the guinea pig whose eyes were still tightly shut. Maybe they weren't Russian speaking? I can't believe it was my bad pronunciation.

Great, I thought...I won't get much out of these...let's try the cosmonaut.

I tried to make polite conversation with Ivan Ivanovich. I knew his name because it was sewn onto his space suit with along with a flag. He just stared ahead in stony silence. It was creepy. I forgave his bad manners as I thought he must be really concentrating on all the switches and levers in front of him for take-off. Perhaps he didn't speak English and I knew my Russian was somewhat limited.

It was then that the guinea pig opened its eyes and piped up,

'He's a dummy, you dummy!'

I looked more closely at the plastic jawline and shiny hands and suddenly felt rather silly. I remember overhearing the smiley lady telling the floppy haired boy, that when she was young, she didn't realise that the heroes of her favourite television programme were actually puppets. She never saw the strings. Suddenly I knew how she felt!

At least the guinea pig spoke English…that was a start.

'I knew that,' I lied.

'I don't like the take-off…gets me every time.' The guinea pig looked down at her claws and the scratch marks she'd made on the bottom of the cage. She said her name was Eva.

'You mean you've been up into space before?' I asked, incredulously.

The Secret Adventures of Rolo

'Yes several times… the middle bit is alright… the take-off and the re-entry are a bit tricky.'

I must admit I looked at this furry pencil case on legs with new respect, if she really was a seasoned space traveller.

'Don't worry about the mice; they never speak to anyone…I wonder if they are KGB or perhaps they are American secret agents, you never know who you are dealing with these days.'

What an interesting thought! I wondered whether a white mouse could spy or whether it could possibly be bugged!

'What happens next?' I asked the experienced cosmo-guinea pig.

'Look out of the window and tell me what you can see?' Eva replied.

'Well I can see a big round thing…I guess that's Earth where we've just come from.'

'I've heard that it's possible to see The Great Wall of China from here…can you see anything that looks like that?' she said.

I peered out from the porthole again and saw what looked like a chain, linking over a corner of the Earth.

'Yes! I can see it!'

'Quick, let me out of this cage! I want to see it for myself!'

I unfastened the latch and the guinea pig climbed out. The mice didn't look too interested in sightseeing so I bolted the cage door again.

'Hurry, let me stand on your shoulder, we don't have much time!'

I obligingly laid down flat so that Eva could climb up and then I put my paws up on the ledge of the hatch so she could see out from the porthole.

'Wow! See how the Earth curves! See how half is in shadow!' The intelligent guinea pig was very excited to be able to see more than the bars of the cage.

'What happens next?' I asked.

'Oh, we just hang about up here for a while… things will liven up in a minute. The dummy will be programmed to do a few things and, when we get back to Earth, they will do some scientific experiments on our heart rate and so on, to see how we coped with the flight. They need us to run a few tests on us before they send a man up into space. I hear that's coming soon. Naturally it will be a Russian who gets to the Moon first…'

I glanced over at the mice and this last statement made them twitch their whiskers uneasily and swap nervous glances as if they were in silent disagreement with the guinea pig.

'Speaking of the Moon, bet you thought

The Secret Adventures of Rolo

there was the face of a man on it, didn't you?
Look over there!'

I followed the direction Eva was pointing
and then started laughing.

Clear as anything I could see the silhouette
of a bunny on a skateboard! I would never
ever be able to look up at a full moon again
without thinking of this space flight.

Whoah! Suddenly my feet left the ground
and I was floating about in the space capsule!
The mice were bobbing around at the top of
their cage. Eva was on the ceiling! Only Ivan
Ivanovich seemed unmoved by the whole
experience.

'What's happening now?' I shouted to Eva.

'Nothing at all to worry about. Enjoy the
feeling of weightlessness! Try a back flip!' she
encouraged.

I launched myself backwards and was
surprised at the ease with which I turned

full circle and then landed the right way up again. I say landed, although my paws were still dangling in mid-air! This is amazing, I thought. Wouldn't the floppy haired boy love to have a go at this!

'Do you think you can climb down the wall and let us out of our cage so we can join in the fun?' squeaked one of the mice in what I thought sounded a bit like an American accent.

'I'll try. Hold on. It's not easy fighting against gravity! ' I replied, loving the adventure.

I found a few footholds and held on with all my strength as I scaled down the inside of the spacecraft, head first. I was really struggling to remain on the ground and it took all my strength and concentration to grip the bars of the cage and undo the latch again.

Like a cork held down in a bucket of water and suddenly released, the three white mice

The Secret Adventures of Rolo

shot up to the top of the spacecraft and then started floating about in free fall positions. I released my grip on the cage and went up to join them. We were all turning somersaults and giggling and bumping into each other.

Only Ivan Ivanovich didn't join in the fun. I wondered if I should unstrap him too but decided against it. What fun could a plastic man possibly have in a gravity-free zone?

After a while, Eva shouted over the laughter,

'Brace yourselves…it's time to re-enter the Earth's atmosphere.'

Without further warning we all plummeted

to the floor of the space craft and I heard a tremendous whooshing and roaring in my ears. Everything went black for a moment.

Eventually, when the door of the spacecraft was opened, I was first out and jumped up and licked the hand and then under the chin of the surprised scientist who had bent down to open the hatch.

I could hear puzzled discussions amongst the humans as to why the guinea pig and mice were running around on the floor and not still fastened in their cage. Only Ivan Ivanovich was where he should be, his plastic face not giving away any of our secrets.

I decided my best course of action was to run and hide and then get back to the time tunnel as quickly as possible. There was no way I was going to be wired up and monitored in a laboratory experiment! I was on such an adrenalin high.

Yulia met me in the tunnel 'Ground control

to Major Rolo!'

I slept very soundly in my basket for the remainder of the night. I wished I could show the floppy haired boy the bunny on the skateboard, he'd love that! Perhaps he'll see it for himself from the back garden next time there is a full moon.

Opening the kitchen door in the morning, the floppy haired boy said I looked a little spacey.

Chapter 17

Rolo and the X-rays

Over breakfast a few days later, the smiley lady was talking to the floppy haired boy about someone she knew having a CAT scan. I had no idea at all what that meant! I was of course curious. Why not a DOG scan?

She went on to explain to him that it was a fusion of X-rays put through a computer to create detailed images of the inside of the body. Wow!

I went to the forest that night without waiting to be summoned, and asked Athelstan, fount of all knowledge, that very same question. He didn't really know the answer as to why CAT and not DOG, so instead he sent me down the time tunnel to Wurzberg University in Germany in 1895.

The guardian of the time tunnel assured me that a man called Wilhelm Conrad Röntgen

The Secret Adventures of Rolo

would know the answer.

The time tunnel brought me right into a laboratory and I glance around at all the test tubes, flasks and Bunsen burners and then moved closer to see what the scientist was up to on the high bench in the corner of the room.

He had a very alarming, huge, bushy beard and his dark eyebrows were furrowed together in total concentration. I tried to remain invisible under a tall wooden stool.

The scientist seemed to be experimenting with electronic beams in some kind of glass cathode ray tube. He noticed that a fluorescent screen in the laboratory began to glow whenever the tube was turned on. This result surprised Röntgen because he thought that the heavy cardboard surrounding the tube would catch most of the radiation.

He switched off the electric current and made a few notes: he thought this proved that some kind of radiation must somehow travel in space.

The scientist didn't know exactly what he had discovered, so he wrote down the letter X and the word 'radiation'. This experiment proved to him what he already suspected; that X-rays actually penetrate most materials.

Röntgen began to place different things between the tube and the screen, but none of them prevented the screen from glowing. Finally, the scientist placed his hand in between the tube and the screen and the silhouette of his bones was clearly visible on the screen. This was the first X-ray.

He looked up and saw me and called me over, lifting me up onto the tall stool so I could sit and witness this phenomenon close up.

Unfortunately at this point, before I had a chance to ask my question, his wife came in with his lunch. When Mrs Röntgen spotted me she started shouting at me in German, horrified to see a dog in her husband's pristine laboratory which she kept spick and span, and from all the arm waving I gathered that she was very upset that I had interrupted his important research.

Röntgen looked at me apologetically, raising one of those great bushy eyebrows, and Frau Röntgen gathered up her skirts and shooed me outside.

I had to sneak back into the laboratory when neither of them were looking.

He had persuaded Mrs R to put her hand in the box and fortunately they were so absorbed in admiring her wedding ring and the delicate nature of her bones on the screen that I managed to creep past on tiptoes and jump into the fume cupboard to access the time tunnel and get out of there. He saw me out of the corner of his eye and winked.

The Secret Adventures of Rolo

I didn't have the opportunity to ask him about the CAT scan but came to the conclusion that, like William Shakespeare, the wife of the inventor of X-rays didn't much like dogs. Maybe **she** was the one to name the medical process.

I tumbled out at the foot of the oak tree and reported all of this back to Athelstan and he explained to me just how important this discovery was in medical science.

X-rays allowed doctors to look directly through tissues and see broken bones, cavities, and swallowed objects with ease and they could also be used to examine soft tissues. I had just witnessed one of the most useful inventions in medicine. I still didn't know why brain scans were named after cats though. I personally didn't think cats had any brains.

Coincidentally, the following week, the smiley lady announced she had an appointment at a clinic for something called

The Secret Adventures of Rolo

Digital Infrared Thermal Imaging.

She often talked out loud which was helpful to me as it helped me to know what she was up to. She later told the floppy haired boy about it and together they did some research and found that thermal imaging was something that had been developed some hundred years after the invention of X-rays.

'Nothing to worry about' she reassured the floppy haired boy. 'Thermal imaging means that the body can be scanned and then re-scanned three months later for any sign of change in the tissues. This type of X-ray is used as a preventative measure, so I am going along to be scanned to make sure that everything is as it should be on the inside of my body.'

The floppy haired boy was at school at the time of the appointment and so, for reasons previously explained about not being left at home during the day, I went along with her to the clinic and sat in the car whilst she went inside for her scan. Great opportunity to catch up on a bit of sleep as I had been busy lately.

After about half an hour, the smiley lady appeared with a nice lady in a white coat.

'Rolo, would you like to be X-rayed?' the smiley lady asked as she lifted me out. I think it was a rhetorical question.

I was carried into a small consultation room and they closed the door. Then the smiley lady held me firmly underneath my tummy whilst the nice lady in the white coat zoomed a camera on a stand right in to point directly at me.

No one asked me to smile. The whole procedure was all quite painless – in fact I can honestly say I didn't feel a thing.

That evening, the smiley lady shrieked in delight and called the floppy haired boy over to look at her laptop screen. The nice

The Secret Adventures of Rolo

white coated lady had emailed my Digital
Infrared Thermal Image over. I jumped up
on the smiley lady's lap to have a better look.
They were both laughing and saying I looked
really psychedelic. Then they were saying
something about, 'wasn't it a shame that dogs
can't see colour, only black and white.'

I don't know what they were talking about
because I **can** see colour. I'm not like other
dogs as you may have already worked out.
However, this drawing is in black and white
so you can see an ordinary dog's eye view.
I felt slightly better about the whole X-ray
thing because I had now had the first official
'dog scan'.

The Secret Adventures of Rolo

Dog Blog #10 — According to Rolo

The smiley lady and I were walking back from our usual walk over the fields and, just as we were about to cross our road to go home, we heard the unmistakable squeal of car brakes followed by a thud. One of the local cat mafia who is the torment of my life had been knocked down.

The poor driver stopped and spoke to the smiley lady. He didn't see the running cat until it was too late; the silly thing just shot out in front of him and ran across the road. Luckily the cat ran off straight away, so they didn't think it was too badly hurt.

The smiley lady thought she knew who the cat belonged to and did some detective work. Luckily the owner was traced and she came home from work to try to find her injured cat. She was wandering around calling and peering everywhere, but the injured cat was nowhere to be seen.

The smiley lady had the bright idea of using me as a sniffer dog to locate the wounded cat, and she attached my lead and off we went to the heavily shrubbed area outside the house of the cat owner. I could smell it, but the smiley lady wouldn't let me off my lead so I nearly pulled her through a privet hedge to get to it.

'I think your cat's in there!' said the smiley lady pointing to the bush. I was jumping up and down like a yoyo on the lead, whimpering

The Secret Adventures of Rolo

and very pleased with my detective work.

'Mr Raffles! Mr Raffles!' the owner called.

'I don't think he's there; he's not answering me,' the distraught cat owner added.

'I think if Rolo and I exit the scene, if I'm not mistaken, you will find your injured cat keeping a very low profile under those bushes,' said the smiley lady.

And so I was dragged reluctantly home. And, yes, Mr Raffles is alive and well and has resumed his habit of making my life a misery.

Chapter 18

Rolo and the Amesbury Archer

The smiley lady visits primary schools. I usually go with her as I don't really like being left home alone during the day and can be a bit naughty if left to my own devices.

Today we drove west to Amesbury, which is on the way to Salisbury. It was a very hot day and so the nice lady on the reception desk in the school said that, rather than leave me in the car with the windows open, I could sit quietly at her feet whilst the smiley lady went to work, talking to the junior children and inspiring some creative writing.

I sat obediently on the floor of the reception area tied with my lead to the nice office lady's swivel chair and I closed my eyes and put my head on my paws. Always chasing sleep, me. I am permanently tired from my night time adventuring. Dog tired.

Glancing over at the circular wall of the foyer of the school, I noticed a rather interesting wall painting showing a man with a pony tail holding a long bow, and, next to him, a somewhat taller version of me. I stared at the mural and drifted off to sleep, dreaming of barrows.

When the smiley lady came back to the reception area she noticed the wall painting and asked the nice lady about it.

'Oh, that's the Amesbury Archer,' she said. 'When they excavated the area twelve years ago, prior to putting down the foundations for the building of the school, the work men found what they assumed to be Roman relics. Building work was halted and archaeologists called in, and after a whole day of gentle scraping and digging, the grave of a man was revealed.

This turned out to be far more exciting than Roman remains and much older. The skeleton had a bow beside him and a group

The Secret Adventures of Rolo

of arrow heads, lots of artefacts and, most unusually, a golden hair clasp that seemed to be one of a pair.

The bones were tested for age and the pottery remnants dated him back to the Beaker People; the first settlers of Britain some 4000 years ago.'

The smiley lady was fascinated. So was I! I wanted to know what happened to the dog in the picture as no one had mentioned the skeleton of a dog being discovered.

I heard the receptionist telling the smiley lady that it was thought the Amesbury Archer came from the Alps, the area we know today as Switzerland. How could anyone possibly know that? What did they find? A triangular chocolate wrapper in his pocket or perhaps remnants of museli in his stomach?

I'd have to ask Athelstan.

The Secret Adventures of Rolo

'A bit of ancient history for you, Little Pup,' said the wise gatekeeper of the time tunnel when I next had the opportunity to visit him.

'The Bronze Age was a very important time between the Stone Age and the Iron Age and it lasted about fifteen hundred years throughout Europe. Travellers came to Britain from the continent bringing drinking vessels with strange markings which showed Minoan influences meaning the people had some link with Crete. Some of these cups have been found in burial sites. That's why these peaceful travellers, who mixed well with the Stone Age inhabitants of Britain, are now known as the Beaker People.

It was thought they came to this area of the South West that we are in, which we now call Wessex, because of the warmer climate for grazing livestock, and the rich availability of tin and copper underground which proved to be very useful when mixed, as it could be used for weapons and cooking pots and jewellery, hence the name 'Bronze Age'.

I took in about half of this information and asked Athelstan if he knew anything about the Amesbury Archer's dog and what happened to him?

'Would you like to find out first hand?' the guardian asked.

'You bet!' I didn't need asking twice!

The next thing I knew, I emerged blinking in the daylight on to what I could only assume to be Salisbury Plain.

In the distance I could see a collection of large stones leaning against each other and that gave me a bearing. This place must be close to Stonehenge.

The wind whistled straight across the bleak landscape, ruffling my short fur coat. It was pretty cold. I thought Athelstan said prehistoric Wessex was supposed to be warm!

I saw a huddled band of men and women coming towards me. They didn't look war-like at all; in fact they looked rather sad. The next thing that struck me was that they were wearing homespun clothes, not the animal pelts of their predecessors.

I remembered what Athelstan had said: these people knew how to weave. The women were wearing short tunics over long woollen skirts. The men wore knee-length wrap-around skirts, or kilt-like woollens, and cloaks over their tunics. The other thing that struck me was that the appearance of the men was not at all wild looking and hairy; all were clean-shaven, with their long hair tied back and some covered their hair with woollen hats, a forerunner of the boy with floppy hair's beanie.

One of the women noticed me and threw a scrap of spelt bread from her apron in my general direction. I eagerly gobbled it up. I thought I would follow them to see where they were going and fell into step just behind.

I noticed that they were carrying a variety of copper knives, deer antlers, flint arrowheads and boars tusks between them, but again it struck me that they didn't look as if they were going into battle.

I followed them to a small clearing where a barrow stood. Athelstan had explained to me that the barrows which dot the downs of Wiltshire were actually small burial mounds dug into the chalk and mostly dating from this time period.

The sound of the wind whipping was the only noise and when the wind suddenly dropped I could hear the pitiful howl of a dog sounding as if it was in pain. Naturally curious, I skirted around the mound and recognised the four-legged companion of the Amesbury Archer, the one from the wall painting, and she was crying as if her heart would break.

The Secret Adventures of Rolo

I went over and sniffed her mouth and wagged my tail vigorously to show I meant no harm. This was doggy code easily understood in any time period. She looked up through her wet lashes and I thought her big brown eyes were drowning in their own tears.

'My master's no longer for this life,' she sobbed, and I moved closer to comfort her, whining in sympathy.

Her tail remained low and her eyes downcast. I went round to the entrance of the burial mound and peeped inside. The mound was held up by a timber frame and in the middle lay an earthen slab, draped in woven cloth.

Lying on the slab was a man dressed in quality woollen clothes with shield guards on his arms and his long hair tied back showing his features to be lean and handsome. He looked like he was asleep. The man had a bronze dagger strapped to his chest with a leather string and his bow lay by his side. The floor of the mound was filled with all manner of everyday objects: flint arrow heads, cups, bowls, boars tusks, deer antlers.

'Another soul heading to the afterlife,' I thought to myself, remembering the Pharaoh and trying to compare the timescale. I went back outside and stood close to the grieving dog.

'He was a good master, and before he died of his arrow wound he said,

'Flint, take this golden hair clasp and give it to Arcane as a token of my love. She lives in the next settlement. I will keep the other and she will know we were meant to be a pair.

'So now I have this piece of gold, and no master. What am I to do? They're coming to seal the mound now.'

I turned and saw the band of mournful folk enter the mound and come out again empty handed, having deposited in the burial chamber the objects they had been carrying.

It seemed quite obvious to me. 'Well you'd better fulfil your master's last request,' I said to poor Flint, as kindly as I could. 'I'll come with you.'

We scampered to the next settlement, over rough terrain and the sight that met us was a crowd witnessing the promising of a young, long-haired woman to a stocky man with a long bow hanging across his broad shoulders.

'That's Arcane there…and that's Torvig if I'm not mistaken,' whispered Flint in disbelief.

'He and my master were both archers and they often competed with each other to see who was the finest bowman. Some say Torvig killed my master but I can't say that for sure.'

Hmm, I thought, 'Looks like they weren't

The Secret Adventures of Rolo

only rivals in sport', but I kept that thought to myself. Instead I said,

'Right then, probably not the best time to give the bride your late master's love token; look, she's already wearing a hair clasp. Give it here' and I pressed the clasp around Flint's rope collar instead.

'There, it looks much better on you!' I said, trying to cheer her up.

'Look, I'd better get back to my own people,' I said casually, and she asked if she could come with me as her life here was over.

This was awkward. I hadn't mentioned that I was a time travelling dog and that I needed to journey four thousand years into the future, so I said 'probably best you stay here' allowing her to think I came from a less friendly settlement over the Plain. I watched her lope off with her tail drooping.

I found the entrance to the time tunnel quite

easily and jumped in.

'Who's that with you?' asked Yulia, holding up her lantern for a better look, as a dark shadow blocked the light from the entrance.

Flint had followed me, and she had to bend quite low to peer into the tunnel as she had such long legs. The lantern light caught the golden clasp on her collar and it glistened in the dark.

'Rolo you know that you can't bring someone from another time with you. She won't be able to exit at the other end and she'll be trapped in the tunnel.'

Flint looked downcast and started backing out from the tunnel entrance.

'I can't come with you, wherever you are going,' she said sadly, then added, 'Wait! Before you go, please take the golden clasp. You've been really kind and I don't know what else to do with it. If I keep it, someone from the settlement will steal it. My master's burial mound will have been sealed by now so I can't return it to him, so please, I insist, strange dog, you take it.'

There was nothing else for it. I held Yulia's lantern carefully in my teeth whilst Yulia clambered on my back and undid the clasp as Flint's beautiful and noble head filled the tunnel entrance. Yulia admired the fine gold as she inspected it in the lamp light and then she reached up and stroked Flint's nose sympathetically.

We said our farewells. The dog's sad face disappeared from the end of the tunnel.

When we got back to the Athelstan tree, Yulia gave me the clasp. I didn't know what to do with it, because if I took it home the smiley lady or the floppy haired boy would find it.

'Leave it here with me, then,' said Athelstan when I explained my dilemma.

So I hid the clasp in the mossy ground between the tree roots at the base of the oak tree.

As far as I know, it's still there. So if you are ever up in the forest and you think you have found the Athelstan tree, look very carefully amongst the tree roots without treading on his toes. You never know what treasure you might find!

Dog Blog #11 — According to Rolo

It's been quite a hot summer, and my favourite way to cool off is with a dip in the River Kennet. There

are shallow bits where I wade in
and drink, that's when I'm with the
smiley lady.

If I'm with the floppy haired boy he
throws a stick into the deeper bits
of the river and is amazed that I
jump straight in and swim and bring
him back the stick.

I'm great at 'fetch' but I'm not
very good at 'give' so he knows
now to throw a second stick and
therefore I will drop the first and
go and retrieve the second. It's a
great game.

Today we were walking along the
banks of the Kennet where I
usually jump in, and I forgot
that I was with the smiley lady.
I threw myself into the water and
was surprised to find it was a bit

The Secret Adventures of Rolo

deeper than usual. Two men appeared around the river bend with long rubber waders on, right up to the tops of their legs.

I think they were doing something about monitoring the state of the river and one of them picked me up by the scruff of my neck and dropped me unceremoniously on the river bank. How very undignified!

'Sorry, love, I thought your little dog was drowning,' said one of the men in waders when the smiley lady caught up with us.

The smiley lady said it was okay and that I was actually a good swimmer. She asked them what they were doing in the river, whilst I shook myself dry on the bank.

287

'We're counting the trout that
we released earlier this year
upstream. We had to save the trout
when the river flooded its banks in
the Spring and now we're seeing how
far they have migrated and whether
they've grown.'

I thought to myself, I can help you
with that! So I jumped back in and
resurfaced with a trout flopping
across my jaws and dropped it
gently in the shallow tray of water
next to the very surprised men.

The smiley lady sat down on the
bank and watched in delight as I
kept jumping in and bringing out
more trout to count and measure,
to the amazement of the men who
rapidly filled their clipboard.

Then they tipped the bath full

of trout carefully back into the river.

I know the smiley lady was thinking 'shame, I wouldn't have minded one of those for my tea.'

Never mind smiley lady, I'll fetch you one someday when the Environmental Agency aren't looking.

Dog blog #12 According to Rolo

I was down in the town with the smiley lady and Summer School was on. She remembered that she wanted to go to hear an organ recital in the college chapel. Then she remembered she had me with her.

'Well-behaved dogs are allowed,' said the young lady at the entrance to the chapel.

We went inside and people were smiling at me. It's a huge church where people sit round the sides and face each other which is bit more unusual than churches I've been to before. I settled down at the smiley lady's feet in the boxed in pew and lay down on the wooden floor with my head between my paws.

The smiley lady started giggling. She was listening to the organist announcing what he was going to play and one of the pieces was called 'The Cat Suite'. I think she was fervently hoping there were no

The Secret Adventures of Rolo

cat noises imitated in the music!

She needn't have worried. I cocked
an ear up at the crescendos and
dozed during the pianissimos
and all in all it was a very
pleasant way to spend a lunchtime.
Afterwards, I went to be introduced
to the organist because he has
a Jack Russell at home and he
couldn't believe he had one in the
audience. I am a very cultured dog.

The Secret Adventures of Rolo

Chapter 19

Rolo and the Art Thief

I knew the smiley lady was interested in art history. She always reads articles about paintings in the Sunday magazines. There was a bookcase upstairs full of art books. None of her children were terribly excited about the idea of traipsing around London looking at paintings; except the middle one, the one with the house rabbit.

Today she tried to engage the floppy haired boy in a conversation about Flemish paintings and he had a pained expression on his face. Suddenly my ears pricked up when I overheard her say,

'Did you know that Brueghel the Elder always painted dogs in his pictures? Then the great British portrait painters like Gainsborough and Stubbs…they painted dogs in their pictures too…'

The floppy haired boy pushed his chair
back with an exaggerated rolling of his eyes
and went into the kitchen and opened the
fridge door. The smiley lady gave up on
her educating mission as she knew she was
flogging a dead horse.

'There's the same food in there as yesterday,
I haven't been shopping yet,' she said in
exasperation.

He took the orange juice out from the fridge
door and went to drink it from the carton. A
raised eyebrow from the smiley lady through
the doorway made him think again. He went
to the cupboard and got out a glass. His
hand hovered over the dog biscuit tin. I hung
around hopefully.

Well, even if the floppy haired boy wasn't
interested in doggy paintings, I was.

I thought I'd do a bit of research myself and
then wait until they were going out and
take myself off to London via the Chilvester

Passage to see these masterpieces for myself.

I recalled that the Chilvester Passage came out at St Martin in the Fields on the corner of Trafalgar Square which was very handy because that was exactly where the National Gallery was located.

There was a concert in the redundant church on Sunday evening. The smiley lady and floppy haired boy had gone out to supper with non dog-friendly people and so I was walked early and left home alone. It suited me just fine.

I sneaked into the church through the main door unseen by the admiring audience who were completely absorbed by Rachmaninov's Piano Concerto No.2 being amazingly executed by a young pianist. I nearly settled down in the audience, being a classical music fan, but then I remembered why I was there.

I managed to sneak under the grand piano, having retrieved the tape recorder from the

Lady Chapel.

Oops, I nearly brushed the leg of the pianist, as his feet softly worked the pedals.

I just had to wait for a loud bit in the music so I could switch on the tape recorder to play the chimes.

There was a pause in the movement, and the sound of screeching bagpipes suddenly filled the otherwise silent nave.

I dropped the tape recorder with a clatter and quickly turned it off with my paw, and then held my breath trying to make myself invisible underneath the piano stool.

A few people were looking around to try to work out where the terrible din had come from. Hopefully they would think it was some inconsiderate teenager's ringtone who had forgotten concert etiquette about turning his mobile phone off. Then I realised there weren't actually any teenagers in the audience!

Phew, I think I got away with it. I could hear my heart banging against my rib cage as loudly as a bass drum. I counted to ten and flipped the cassette over and when the pianist reached another crescendo I pressed 'play' again.

Ding, ding, ding the chimes rang out all the way to twelve and thankfully the sound was disguised by the music.

After what seemed like an eternity the outline of the dog on the wall went blurry and I could leave the safety of the piano stool and scurry down the passage, turning the machine off and leaving it just inside the entrance.

No sign of Yulia, but I knew the way well enough in the dark and soon found my nose pressed up against the cold metal of The Talbot Café sign.

The Secret Adventures of Rolo

I let myself out quietly and dropped to the pavement. I glanced both ways and then quickly crossed Duncannon Street to enter the square. Nelson, as usual, had his back to me.

Being a Sunday evening I suppose it wasn't quite as busy as during the week. I disturbed a few pigeons as I crossed the square, under the watchful eye of a man on a horse on a plinth that I hadn't noticed before, and darted up the shallow steps to the famous building with pillars along the front and a dome on the roof: London's National Gallery. How the smiley lady would have loved to have been with me!

The gallery had been closed to the public since six o'clock that evening and a small door to the left side of the main entrance in the portico had been left open for the nightly team of cleaners.

They were easily spotted in their bright yellow overalls. I had to take a quick look at the floor plan on a large stand in the foyer. Luckily the coast was clear and I consigned the route to memory.

I was heading to the second floor as I wanted to see these Brueghel paintings in room 28, the Flanders room.

I kept to the right hand side and bounded up the wide marble staircase under the dome and wrinkled my nose at the large urns on either side of the stairs, as they were overflowing with highly scented flowers.

On through the double doors into the Central Hall and then into Room 30 with all its Velasquezes and Murillos, the most easily recognisable of the Spanish painters. The smiley lady would be impressed at my recognition!

Nothing for me in here, although I did poke my head into Room 31 to see van Dyck's enormous portrait of Charles l on horseback which dominated the room. Alas not a dog

The Secret Adventures of Rolo

painting to be seen.

Aha! At last. Room 14 Jan Gossaert's Adoration of the Kings 1510-1515. Two dogs and one a Spaniel. In the same room I saw a different version of the same subject by Jan Breughel the Elder dated 1598 and this one had two dogs in it too.

I had come to the right place. I cut through Room 29 which was full of Rubens' fleshy women and I had to smile when I saw 'Busty Bertha' (well that's what the smiley lady calls her anyway). At last I was in Room 28 where all the Jan Breughel paintings owned by the National Gallery were grouped together.

It's a small room with red walls and the first thing that struck me about these canvases is that they were very small and hung quite high up. Well, too high for a Jack Russell to see anyway.

Now I'd come all this way to see the dogs in these paintings and I wasn't going to let a

The Secret Adventures of Rolo

little thing like height stop me in my mission.

I went back into the Rubens room and saw a chair by the door, presumably for a gallery attendant to sit in during opening hours whilst on duty, keeping the visitors from touching the paintings or from taking photographs with a flash.

With a nod to Busty Bertha on the wall, I pushed the chair with all my might and a fair bit of floor scraping, through the door and into the small red gallery. Ah, that was better!

I positioned the chair in front of Sea Storm 1595 and peered at the oil on canvas. Eventually I spotted a tiny dog on the deck of the ailing ship. I jumped down and lined up the chair in front of Landscape with Travellers 1610 and it was easy to spot the big dog next to the main scene. Harbour Scene with Christ Preaching 1597 again had small figures and lots of detail and I thought I saw a dog eating a fish.

The adjacent room was number 27 and it had a wooden bench in the middle of it, for the comfort of weary art lovers to take the weight off their feet, so I left the chair where it was, and hopped up on the central podium to survey the room.

Lots of Dutch church interiors and, funnily enough, every single one of them had dogs in them, ranging in shapes, breeds and sizes. Even Jan van der Heyden's 'A View in Cologne' had dogs in it. I decided I liked the Dutch Masters! Interestingly, most of these interiors had curtains painted in the foreground to draw you into the scene as if it were a stage and you, the theatre goer.

I hid under the wooden bench for a moment, as I heard movement in a nearby room. I couldn't help but think how lucky the cleaners were in their silent wielding of large brooms around the wooden floors, being watched by hundreds of painted faces. The cleaners had the best viewing time of all in empty galleries after hours.

I tried to remember the name of the British painters mentioned by the smiley lady and knew it was Gains something. Underneath the bench, someone had left a floor plan. I opened it out and had a look. Gainsborough! That was it! Whilst I was inside the gallery I thought I would use the opportunity to have a look so I made my way to Room 35.

 I scampered back through Rubens and the Spanish artists and a plethora of Italian and French paintings in subsequent rooms. The only portrait that really caught my eye was Murillo's Don Justino de Neve as he has a large adoring dog sporting an orange ribbon around its neck.

It occurred to me that I was having a private viewing and a whistle stop tour of the history of European art! The smiley lady would be impressed!

Room 35. Sure enough all the portraits by

Thomas Gainsborough appeared to have dogs in them.

These were very large canvases and I didn't need to stand on anything to see them clearly. I stopped in front of each and put my paws up on the posts threaded with rope to keep visitors at a certain distance from the paintings.

Mr and Mrs Andrews, Cornard Wood, John Plampin, Portrait of the Artist, with his Wife and Daughter; all of these featured their dogs. I read on the wall plaque that Gainsborough was a founder member of the Royal Academy. He clearly made pet portraits fashionable in the 18th Century.

I heard a sound and quickly ducked under one of the eight-legged leather viewing benches in the room. I kept very still and started counting the buttons in the upholstery.

A man dressed in cleaners overalls with

The Secret Adventures of Rolo

a baseball cap pulled down over his face hurried past me, looking this way and that, barely glancing at the paintings.

He seemed to be looking for something in particular. He took a piece of paper out of his pocket and unfolded it and read it, then returned it to his pocket once more.

He scurried through Rooms 36 and 40 and I followed him into Room 44, grandly labelled 'Beyond Impressionism' dedicated to Harry and Carol someone or other. The man looked about him furtively. It occurred to me that he didn't even have a broom or feather duster. He probably didn't even work for the cleaning company.

I saw, from the safety of beneath a wooden bench, a large canvas I recognised as The Bathers by Seurat, made up of tiny coloured dots. He didn't even glance at that. I then notice another big loosely painted canvas with a Collie dog in the foreground. The man moved towards that, and then stood in front of a much smaller painting on its left.

He didn't look much like an art lover I thought, from beneath the viewing bench.

Glancing this way and that, the man reached inside his overalls and took out a knife with a retractable blade. I swallowed a gasp.

Extending the sharp blade he put his right hand firmly in the middle of the canvas as if he were about to pluck one of those bright daisies from the jar in the middle of the picture.

The scene was of a cluttered mantelpiece, full of vibrant colour and wonderful loosely painted brush strokes.

With his right hand applying pressure, he scored the painting all the way around the edge, liberating it from its frame. It was all I could do not to cry out!

Why weren't the alarms going off? I looked up at the walls and saw that the only sensors in that room were firmly focused on the more famous 'Bathers', which in all honesty would have been too big to remove easily.

The art thief sat down heavily on the other bench opposite the one I was hiding beneath. I held my breath and stayed perfectly still fighting my terrier shake. He laid the painting down next to him on the wooden surface and started to roll it carefully. That's when I noticed there was a painting on the other side!

He was so intent on his task that he didn't seem to register this important and exciting discovery.

Stowing the rolled canvas inside his overalls, with another furtive glance around to make sure no-one was watching, he went out through the end door.

As I left the room, I glanced up at the empty space and quickly read the label imaginatively entitled 'The Mantelpiece' by

The Secret Adventures of Rolo

Eduard Vuillard. It was the first painting to be displayed by a living artist in the National Gallery when it opened in 1917, so the label said.

All of which was immaterial now, unless I could catch up with the thief and recover the painting!

I followed the man a few seconds behind to avoid detection. He hurried through Room 45 and I looked up at the bright splash of yellow and saw Van Gogh's Sunflowers waving cheerily. I clattered my paw on the floor grating, not looking where I was going.

I dived under a viewing bench and held my breath. Phew, that was close.

On through Room 46 and we burst through double doors and suddenly found ourselves back on the familiar mosaic tiles leading to the stairs by the Portico entrance.

The side door was still open but no cleaners

could be seen. The art thief exited the building on the right hand side of the main entrance with me in hot, but secret pursuit, his head down and his booty hidden, clutched firmly to his chest inside the borrowed overalls.

He strode on to Trafalgar Square and I thought, not even Nelson can see what he's doing; the great admiral is still facing the wrong way!

The thief stopped abruptly by an ornate lamppost and retrieved the knife once more. With a deft movement of his left hand he removed the cover at the base of the lamp post and stowed the stolen canvas inside. He then quickly pushed the cover back into place with a click and didn't bother to tighten the screw. I watched him cross the square with his head down and stride out towards Charing Cross station.

I waited by the foot of an equestrian statue and wondered what on earth I should do next. I had witnessed an art theft, but more to the point I could retrieve the painting!

Without too much further thought, I scampered to the lamp post, opened the hidey hole with ease and removed the rolled up painting carefully carrying it in my teeth as if it were a stick, and then I heard an alarm going off.

It was coming from the National Gallery. I assumed one of the cleaners had noticed the empty space and tell-tale dark rectangle on the wall in Room 44 and raised the alarm.

I heard the familiar 'nee naw' of sirens and didn't want to be caught 'red-pawed' so I panicked and galloped across the square with my 'stick' and put it down on the pavement for a moment whilst I levered open the Talbot Café sign; then holding it open with one paw I picked up the precious roll, climbed inside and bolted as fast as I could down the Chilvester Passage heading homeward.

Luckily the walls were just wide enough to allow me and the rolled-up painting to pass through at great speed in the dark.

When I came out inside the church through the dog shaped hole in the wall, I thought that, after the screeching of sirens: the church seemed comfortingly silent.

I laid the scroll carefully on the Minton floor tiles eager to have a closer look at what I had actually retrieved. Luckily the moon was lending her light through the windows.

I had no idea how to return the painting to the gallery, but I really wanted to have a better look at that sketch I'd only glimpsed on the other side, and then I'd give it back. I promise.

I was trying to imagine what the thief would say when he returned to the lamp post to retrieve his stashed painting, only to find it gone.

I carefully unrolled the canvas and then gasped when I saw the picture. As far as I knew, no-one at the National Gallery was even aware of the secret painting on the reverse side of 'The Mantelpiece'.

The next morning the smiley lady walked me down to the High Street to fetch the daily newspaper which she said she only bought for the crossword. She stopped outside the shop and her eyes widened as she read aloud the glaring headline, that a Vuillard still-life entitled 'The Mantelpiece' had been stolen from the National Gallery after closing time sometime yesterday evening.

We stopped in the redundant church on the way home as the smiley lady said she needed a coffee, and we couldn't help but notice a bit of a commotion within.

The custodian, who had unlocked the church building a little before ten o'clock as usual, for the coffee shop staff to gain access, had found a rough sketch of what looked like a

The Secret Adventures of Rolo

woman sitting and two children playing on the sea shore watched by a Jack Russell. The rolled up canvas had been carefully laid out on the grand piano and weighted down at the corners by four hymn books to keep it flat.

Quite a crowd of Marlborough townsfolk gathered round the piano to take a look at the mystery sketch and to offer up their opinions as to how the picture had got there.

None of their guesses were even close to

the truth; one couple thought it was a late entrant for the local artists' exhibition, and still nobody had even thought to flip it over and look at what was on the other side of the sketch.

'Time to go home, Rolo' said the smiley lady, as she dabbed the coffee and walnut cake crumbs from the corners of her mouth, drained her cup, folded her newspaper and untied my lead from the table leg. I put my head down and trotted out from the church behind her, tail waving like a triumphant flag.

Much as I'd like to have made a gift of 'The Mantelpiece' to the smiley lady, I was sure I had done the right thing and knew that the painting would soon be returned to the National Gallery.

The Secret Adventures of Rolo